GEORGE O'CONNOR

ARTEMIS

WILD GODDESS
OF THE HUNT

A NEAL PORTER BOOK

First Second

New York

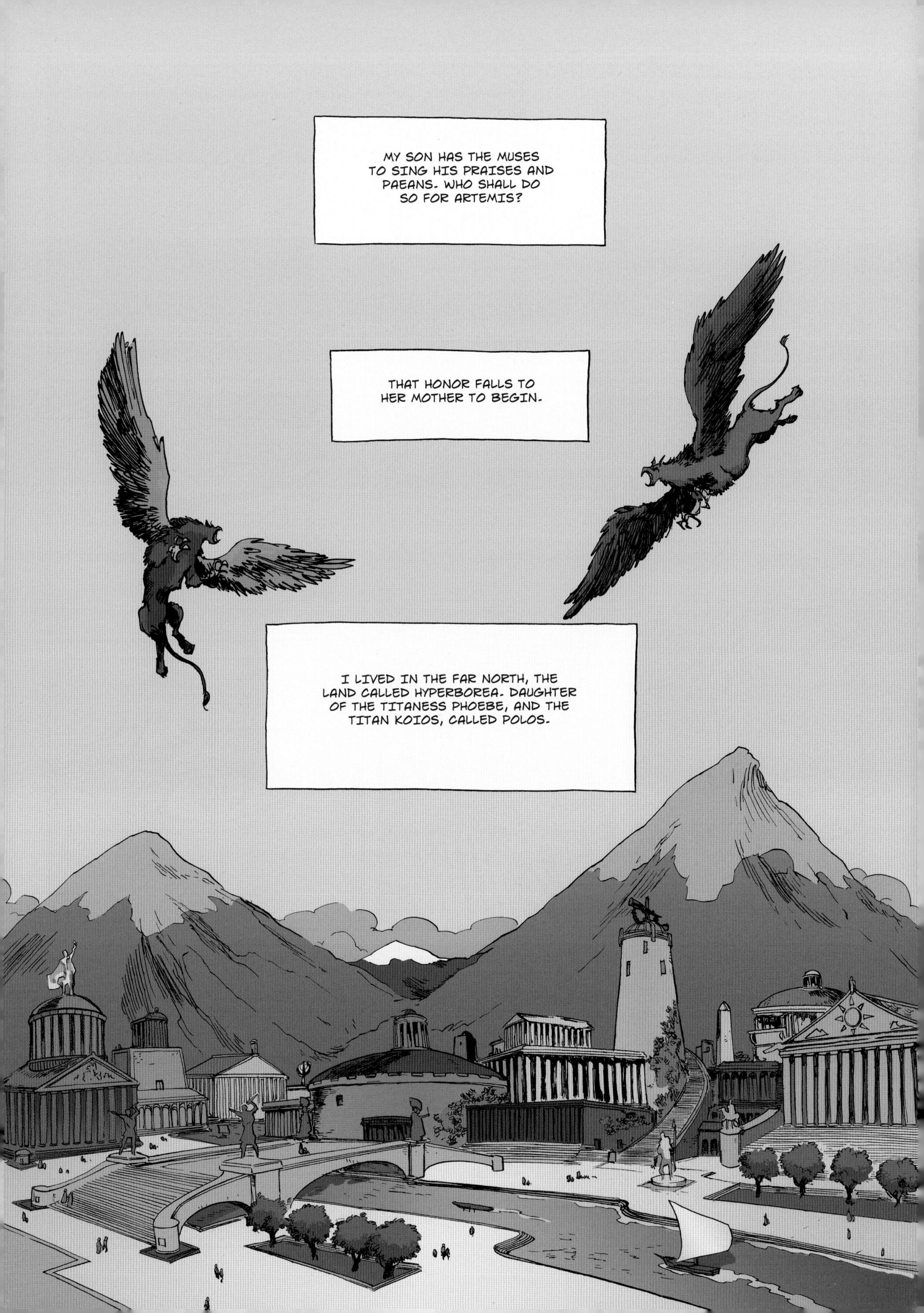
MY SON HAS THE MUSES TO SING HIS PRAISES AND PAEANS. WHO SHALL DO SO FOR ARTEMIS?
THAT HONOR FALLS TO HER MOTHER TO BEGIN.
I LIVED IN THE FAR NORTH, THE LAND CALLED HYPERBOREA. DAUGHTER OF THE TITANESS PHOEBE, AND THE TITAN KOIOS, CALLED POLOS.

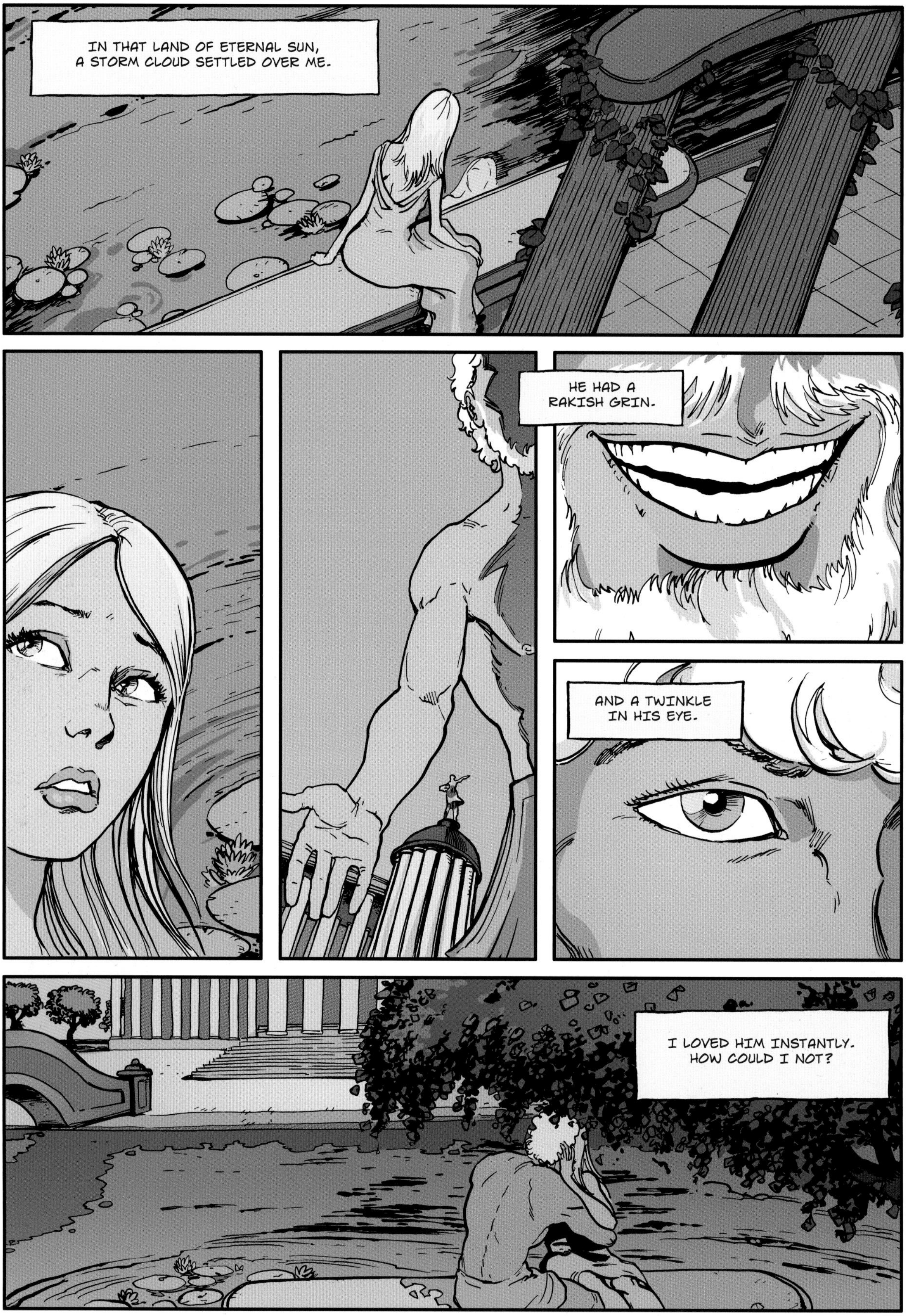
IN THAT LAND OF ETERNAL SUN, A STORM CLOUD SETTLED OVER ME.
HE HAD A RAKISH GRIN.
AND A TWINKLE IN HIS EYE.
I LOVED HIM INSTANTLY. HOW COULD I NOT?

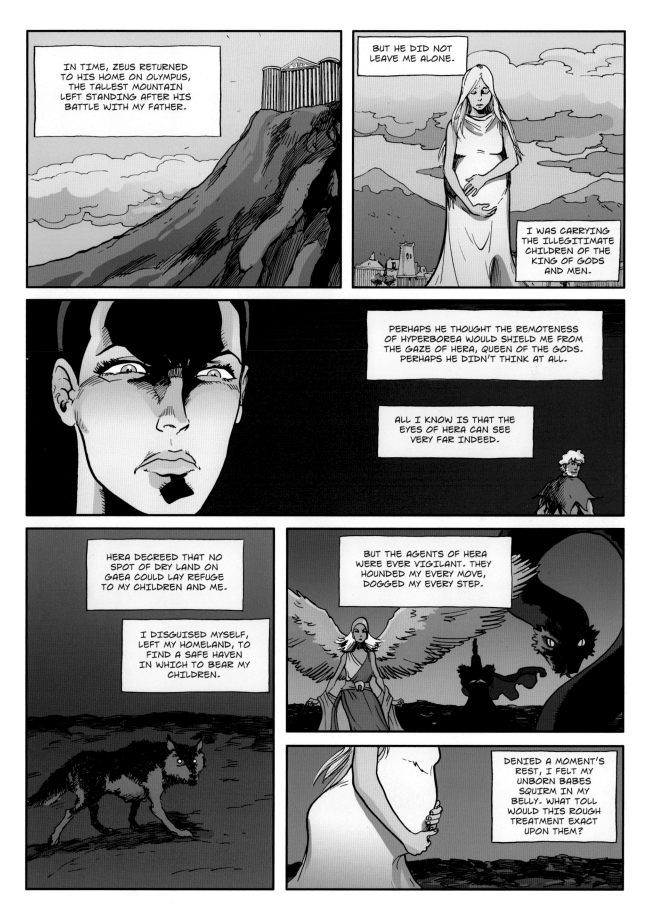

IN TIME, ZEUS RETURNED TO HIS HOME ON OLYMPUS, THE TALLEST MOUNTAIN LEFT STANDING AFTER HIS BATTLE WITH MY FATHER.

BUT HE DID NOT LEAVE ME ALONE.

I WAS CARRYING THE ILLEGITIMATE CHILDREN OF THE KING OF GODS AND MEN.

PERHAPS HE THOUGHT THE REMOTENESS OF HYPERBOREA WOULD SHIELD ME FROM THE GAZE OF HERA, QUEEN OF THE GODS. PERHAPS HE DIDN'T THINK AT ALL.

ALL I KNOW IS THAT THE EYES OF HERA CAN SEE VERY FAR INDEED.

HERA DECREED THAT NO SPOT OF DRY LAND ON GAEA COULD LAY REFUGE TO MY CHILDREN AND ME.

I DISGUISED MYSELF, LEFT MY HOMELAND, TO FIND A SAFE HAVEN IN WHICH TO BEAR MY CHILDREN.

BUT THE AGENTS OF HERA WERE EVER VIGILANT. THEY HOUNDED MY EVERY MOVE, DOGGED MY EVERY STEP.

DENIED A MOMENT'S REST, I FELT MY UNBORN BABES SQUIRM IN MY BELLY. WHAT TOLL WOULD THIS ROUGH TREATMENT EXACT UPON THEM?

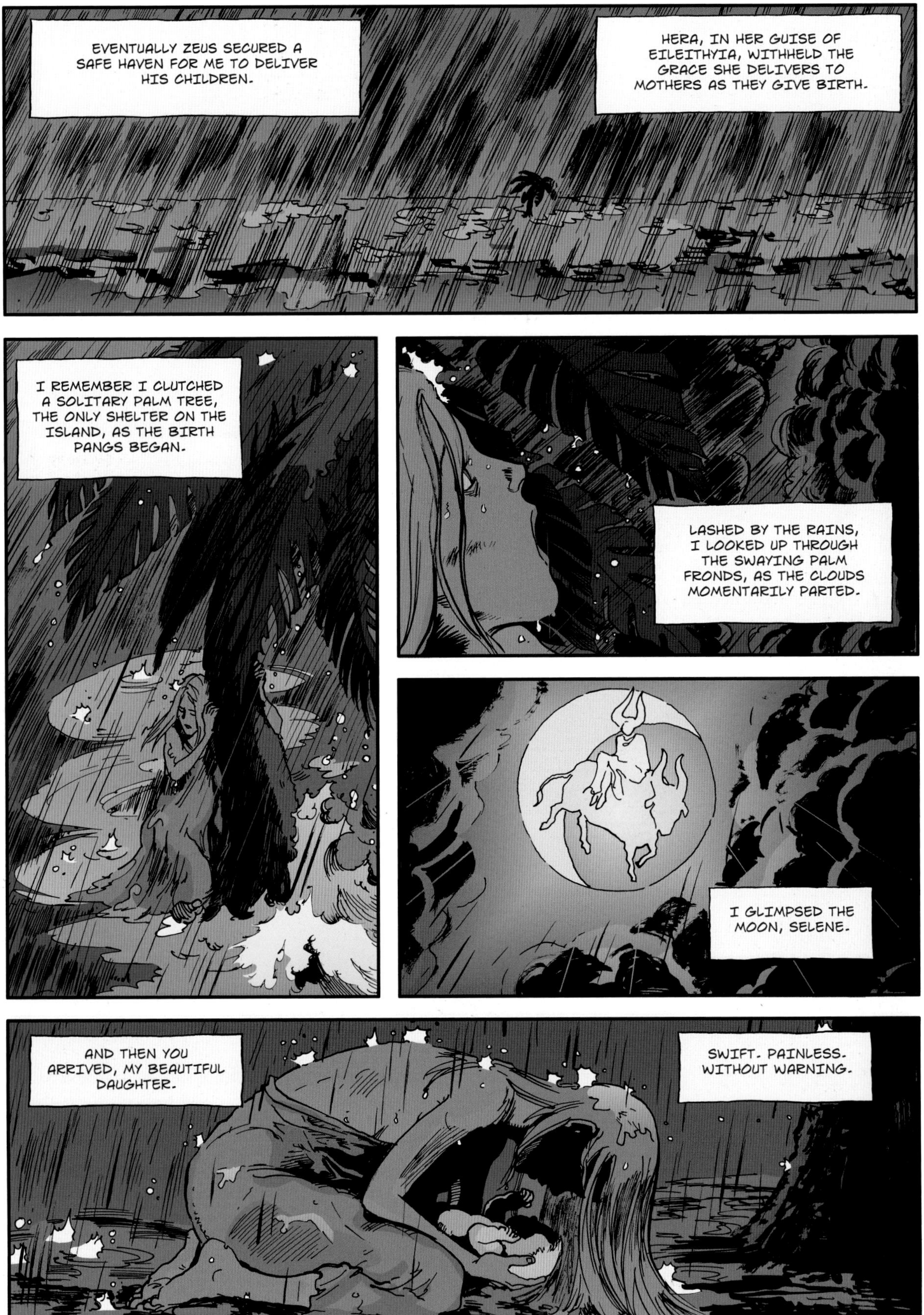
EVENTUALLY ZEUS SECURED A SAFE HAVEN FOR ME TO DELIVER HIS CHILDREN.
HERA, IN HER GUISE OF EILEITHYIA, WITHHELD THE GRACE SHE DELIVERS TO MOTHERS AS THEY GIVE BIRTH.
I REMEMBER I CLUTCHED A SOLITARY PALM TREE, THE ONLY SHELTER ON THE ISLAND, AS THE BIRTH PANGS BEGAN.
LASHED BY THE RAINS, I LOOKED UP THROUGH THE SWAYING PALM FRONDS, AS THE CLOUDS MOMENTARILY PARTED.
I GLIMPSED THE MOON, SELENE.
AND THEN YOU ARRIVED, MY BEAUTIFUL DAUGHTER.
SWIFT. PAINLESS. WITHOUT WARNING.

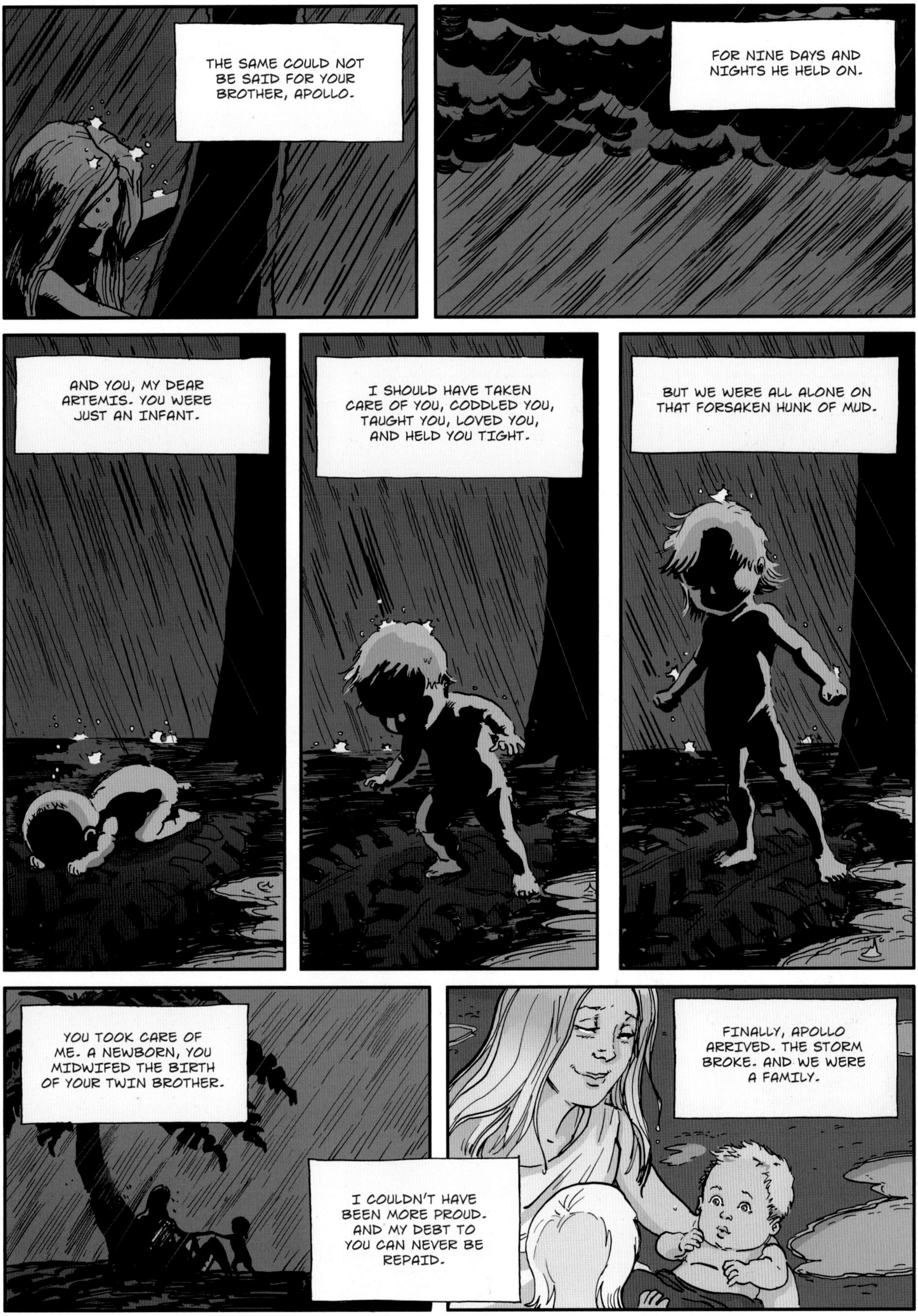
THE SAME COULD NOT BE SAID FOR YOUR BROTHER, APOLLO.
FOR NINE DAYS AND NIGHTS HE HELD ON.
AND YOU, MY DEAR ARTEMIS. YOU WERE JUST AN INFANT.
I SHOULD HAVE TAKEN CARE OF YOU, CODDLED YOU, TAUGHT YOU, LOVED YOU, AND HELD YOU TIGHT.
BUT WE WERE ALL ALONE ON THAT FORSAKEN HUNK OF MUD.
YOU TOOK CARE OF ME. A NEWBORN, YOU MIDWIFED THE BIRTH OF YOUR TWIN BROTHER.
I COULDN'T HAVE BEEN MORE PROUD. AND MY DEBT TO YOU CAN NEVER BE REPAID.
FINALLY, APOLLO ARRIVED. THE STORM BROKE. AND WE WERE A FAMILY.

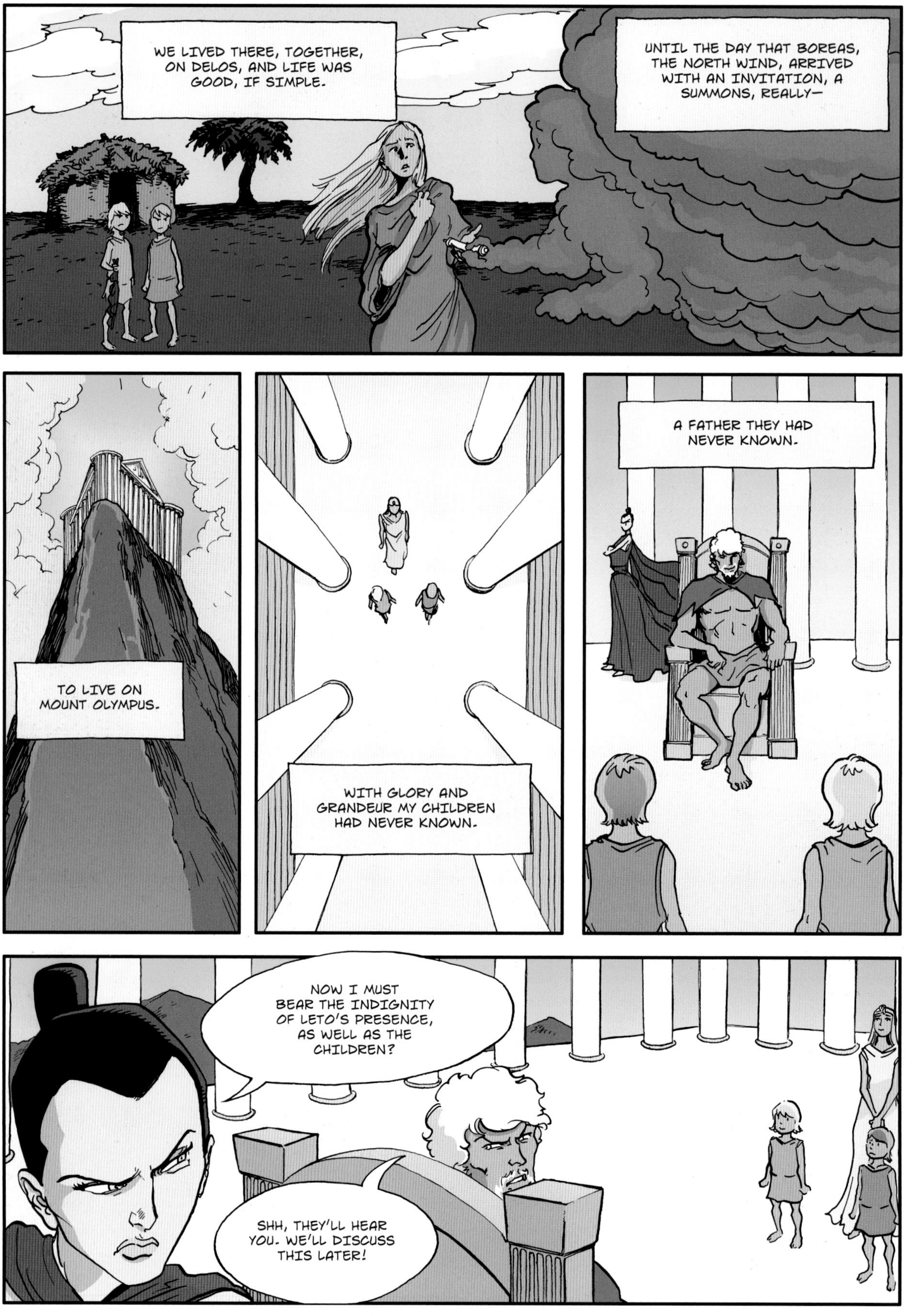
WE LIVED THERE, TOGETHER, ON DELOS, AND LIFE WAS GOOD, IF SIMPLE.
UNTIL THE DAY THAT BOREAS, THE NORTH WIND, ARRIVED WITH AN INVITATION, A SUMMONS, REALLY—
TO LIVE ON MOUNT OLYMPUS.
WITH GLORY AND GRANDEUR MY CHILDREN HAD NEVER KNOWN.
A FATHER THEY HAD NEVER KNOWN.
NOW I MUST BEAR THE INDIGNITY OF LETO'S PRESENCE, AS WELL AS THE CHILDREN?
SHH, THEY'LL HEAR YOU. WE'LL DISCUSS THIS LATER!

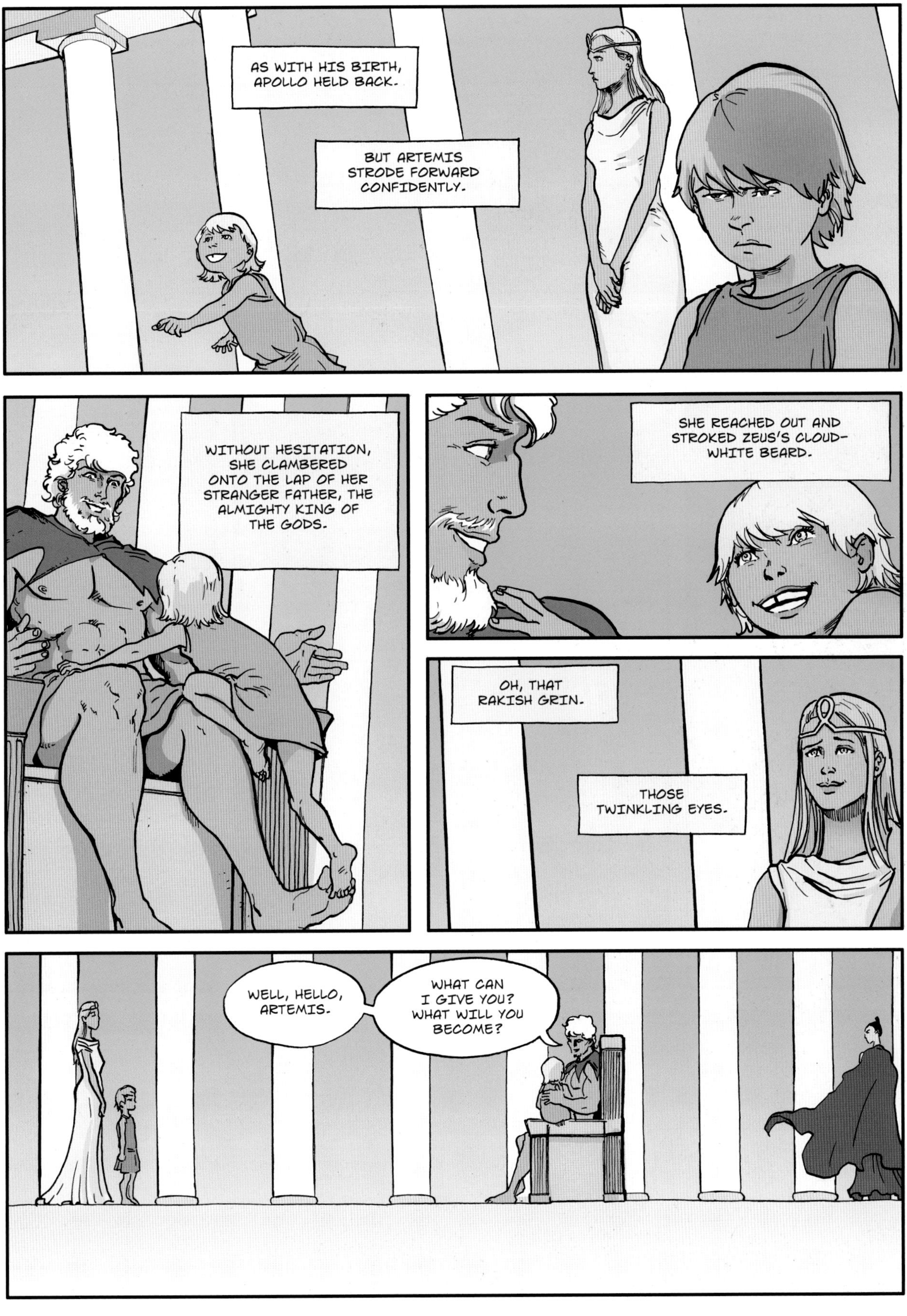
AS WITH HIS BIRTH, APOLLO HELD BACK.
BUT ARTEMIS STRODE FORWARD CONFIDENTLY.
WITHOUT HESITATION, SHE CLAMBERED ONTO THE LAP OF HER STRANGER FATHER, THE ALMIGHTY KING OF THE GODS.
SHE REACHED OUT AND STROKED ZEUS'S CLOUD-WHITE BEARD.
OH, THAT RAKISH GRIN.
THOSE TWINKLING EYES.
WELL, HELLO, ARTEMIS.
WHAT CAN I GIVE YOU? WHAT WILL YOU BECOME?

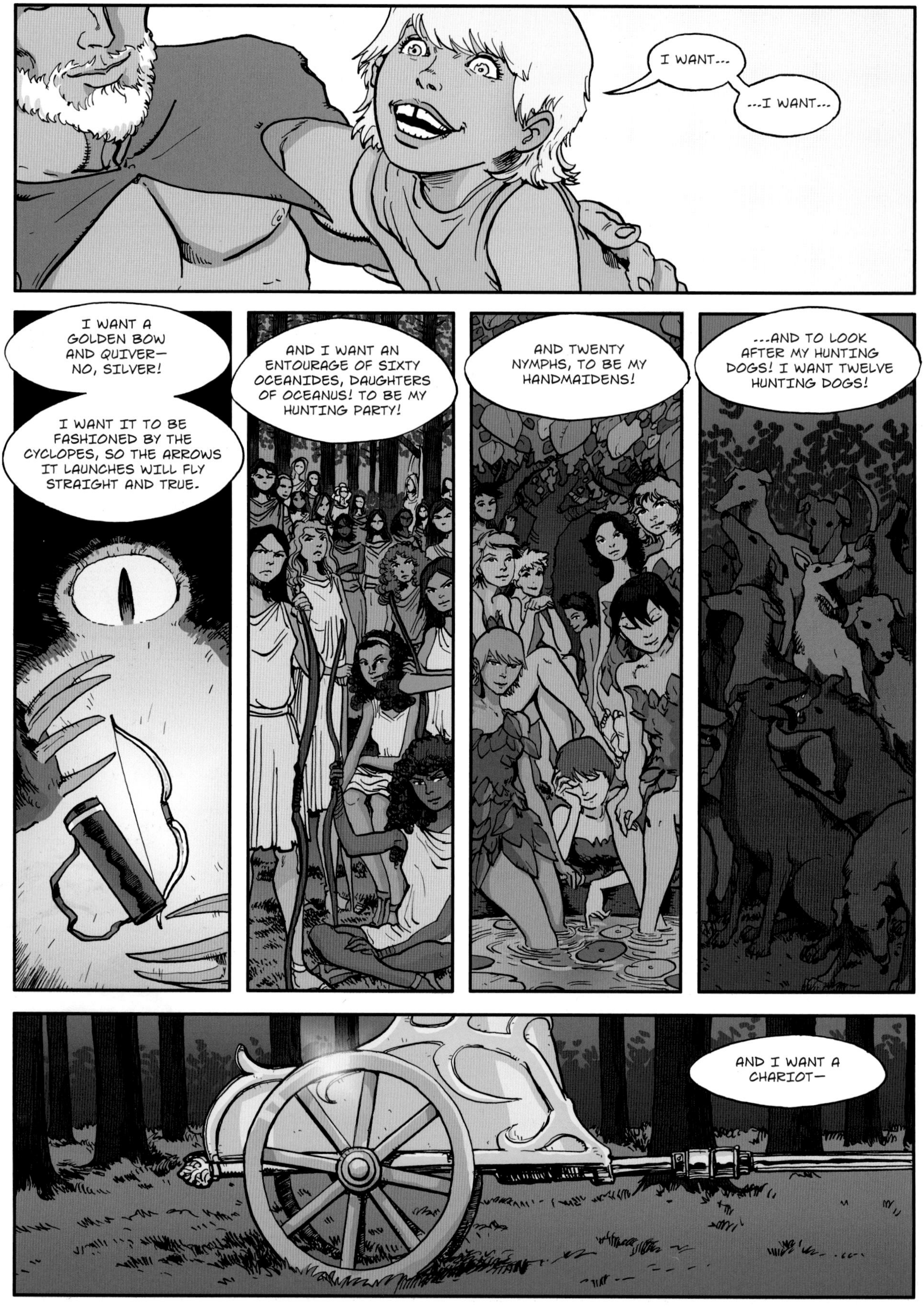
I WANT...
...I WANT...
I WANT A GOLDEN BOW AND QUIVER— NO, SILVER!
I WANT IT TO BE FASHIONED BY THE CYCLOPES, SO THE ARROWS IT LAUNCHES WILL FLY STRAIGHT AND TRUE.
AND I WANT AN ENTOURAGE OF SIXTY OCEANIDES, DAUGHTERS OF OCEANUS! TO BE MY HUNTING PARTY!
AND TWENTY NYMPHS, TO BE MY HANDMAIDENS!
...AND TO LOOK AFTER MY HUNTING DOGS! I WANT TWELVE HUNTING DOGS!
AND I WANT A CHARIOT—

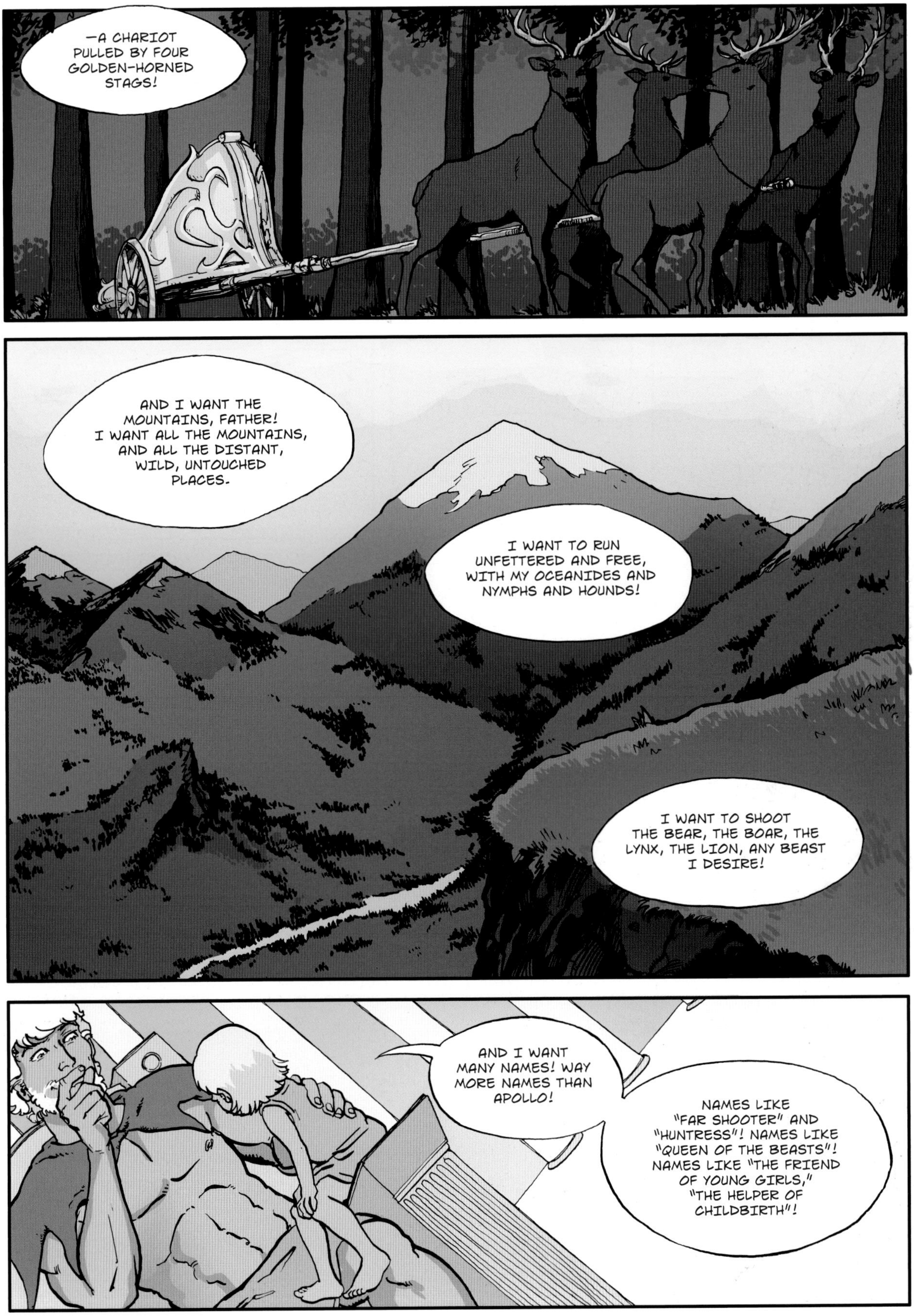
—A CHARIOT PULLED BY FOUR GOLDEN-HORNED STAGS!
AND I WANT THE MOUNTAINS, FATHER! I WANT ALL THE MOUNTAINS, AND ALL THE DISTANT, WILD, UNTOUCHED PLACES.
I WANT TO RUN UNFETTERED AND FREE, WITH MY OCEANIDES AND NYMPHS AND HOUNDS!
I WANT TO SHOOT THE BEAR, THE BOAR, THE LYNX, THE LION, ANY BEAST I DESIRE!
AND I WANT MANY NAMES! WAY MORE NAMES THAN APOLLO!
NAMES LIKE "FAR SHOOTER" AND "HUNTRESS"! NAMES LIKE "QUEEN OF THE BEASTS"! NAMES LIKE "THE FRIEND OF YOUNG GIRLS," "THE HELPER OF CHILDBIRTH"!

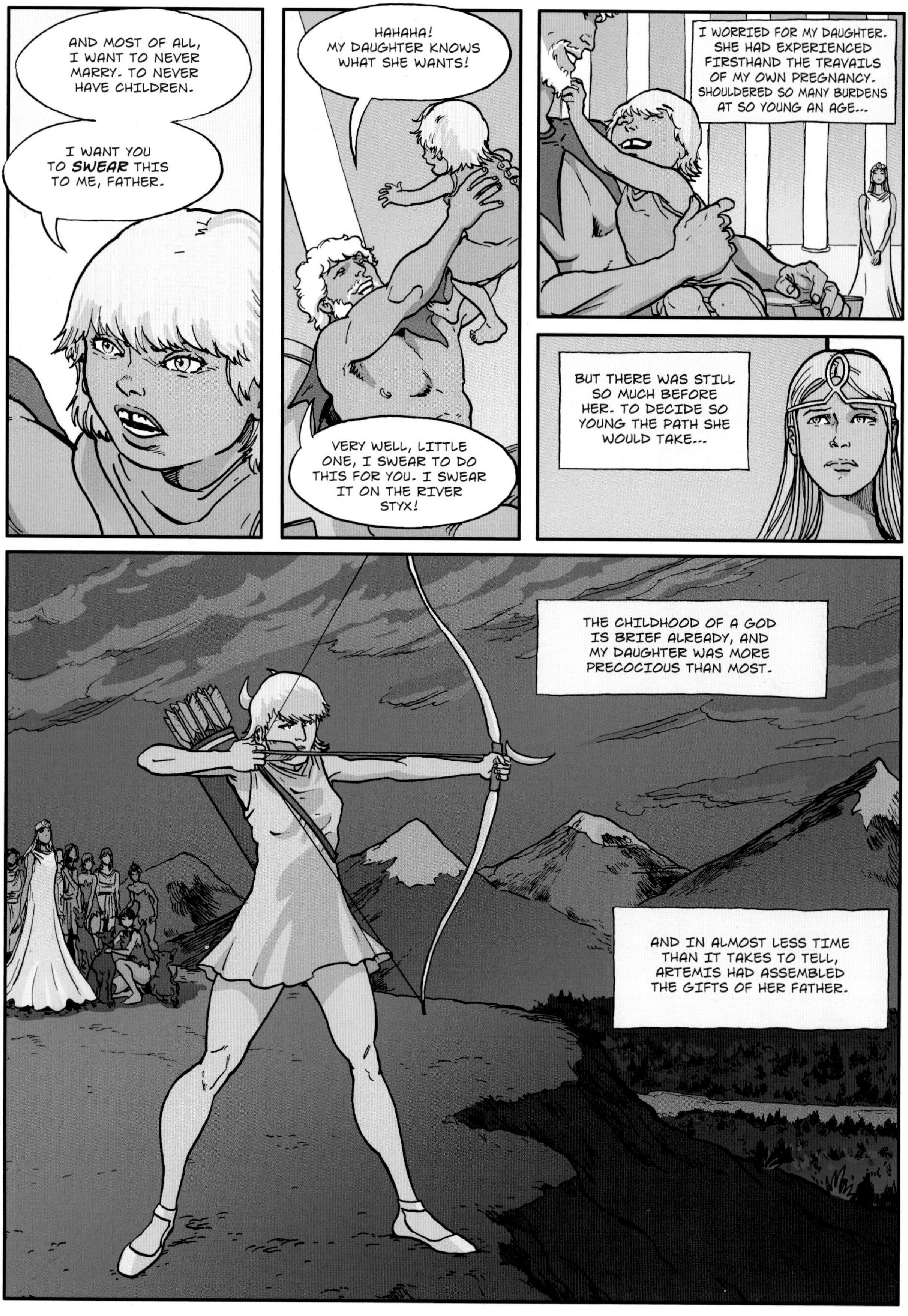
AND MOST OF ALL, I WANT TO NEVER MARRY. TO NEVER HAVE CHILDREN.
I WANT YOU TO SWEAR THIS TO ME, FATHER.
HAHAHA! MY DAUGHTER KNOWS WHAT SHE WANTS!
VERY WELL, LITTLE ONE, I SWEAR TO DO THIS FOR YOU. I SWEAR IT ON THE RIVER STYX!
I WORRIED FOR MY DAUGHTER. SHE HAD EXPERIENCED FIRSTHAND THE TRAVAILS OF MY OWN PREGNANCY. SHOULDERED SO MANY BURDENS AT SO YOUNG AN AGE...
BUT THERE WAS STILL SO MUCH BEFORE HER. TO DECIDE SO YOUNG THE PATH SHE WOULD TAKE...
THE CHILDHOOD OF A GOD IS BRIEF ALREADY, AND MY DAUGHTER WAS MORE PRECOCIOUS THAN MOST.
AND IN ALMOST LESS TIME THAN IT TAKES TO TELL, ARTEMIS HAD ASSEMBLED THE GIFTS OF HER FATHER.

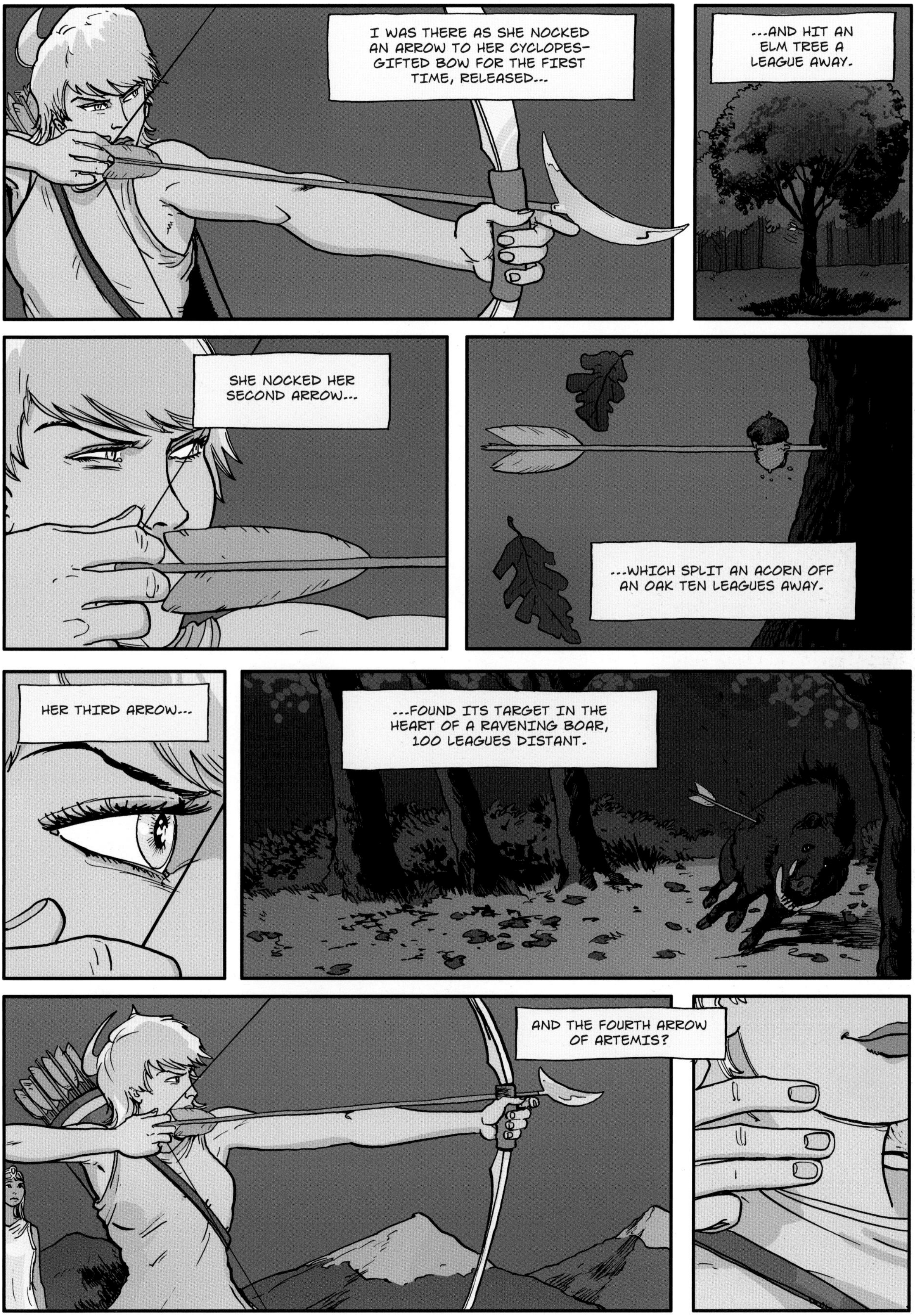
I WAS THERE AS SHE NOCKED AN ARROW TO HER CYCLOPES-GIFTED BOW FOR THE FIRST TIME, RELEASED...
...AND HIT AN ELM TREE A LEAGUE AWAY.
SHE NOCKED HER SECOND ARROW...
...WHICH SPLIT AN ACORN OFF AN OAK TEN LEAGUES AWAY.
HER THIRD ARROW...
...FOUND ITS TARGET IN THE HEART OF A RAVENING BOAR, 100 LEAGUES DISTANT.
AND THE FOURTH ARROW OF ARTEMIS?

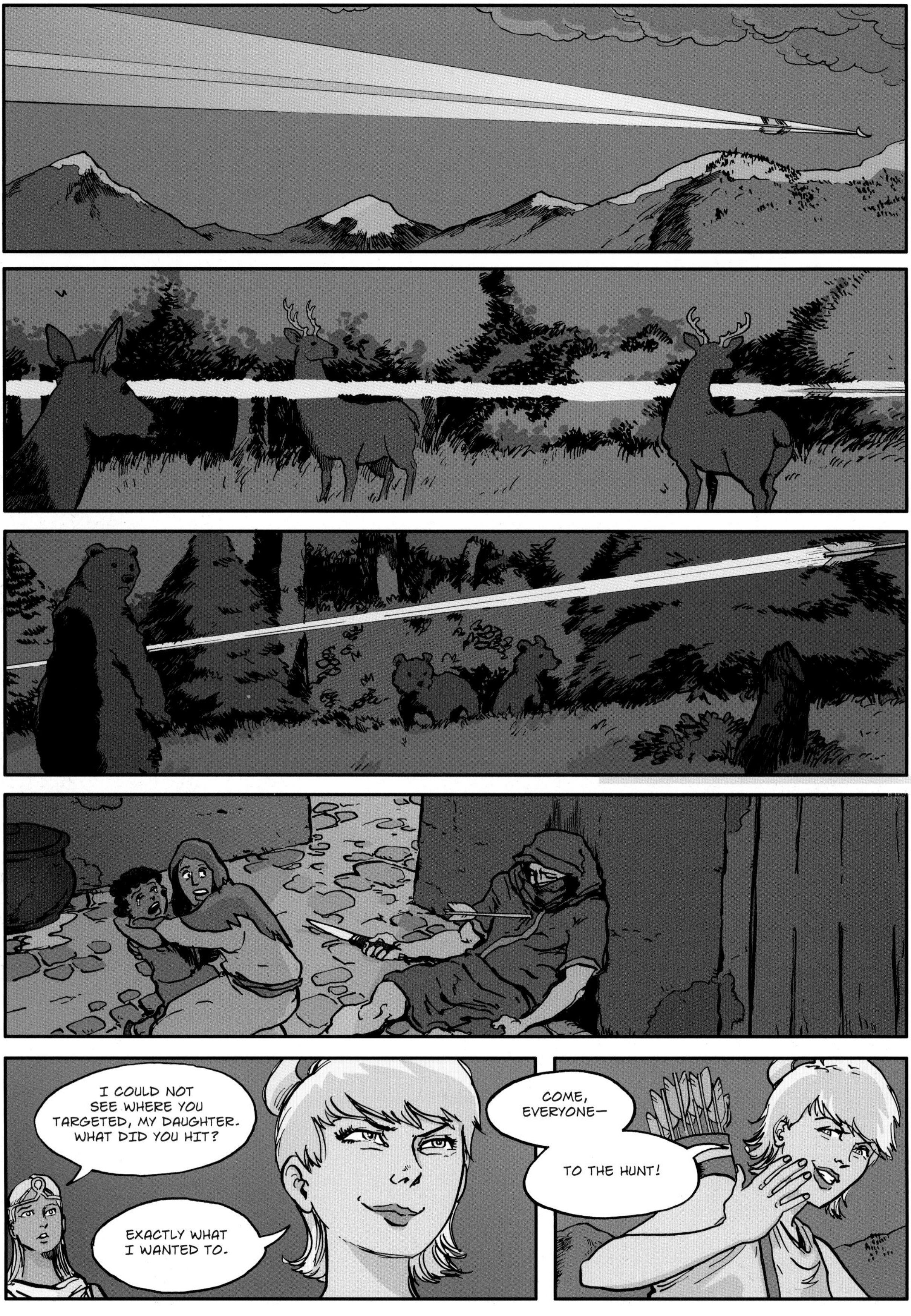
I COULD NOT SEE WHERE YOU TARGETED, MY DAUGHTER. WHAT DID YOU HIT?
EXACTLY WHAT I WANTED TO.
COME, EVERYONE—
TO THE HUNT!

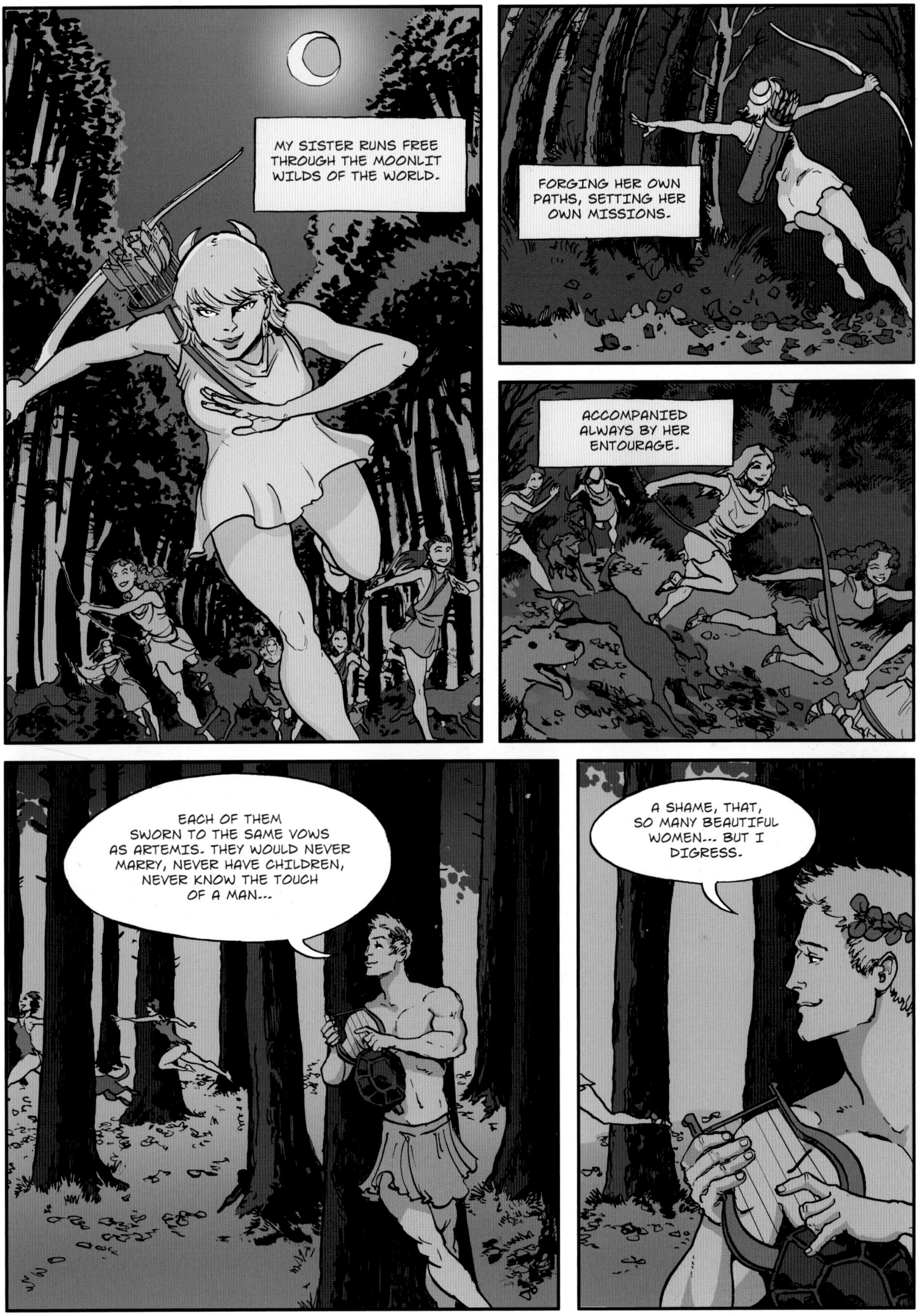
MY SISTER RUNS FREE THROUGH THE MOONLIT WILDS OF THE WORLD.
FORGING HER OWN PATHS, SETTING HER OWN MISSIONS.
ACCOMPANIED ALWAYS BY HER ENTOURAGE.
EACH OF THEM SWORN TO THE SAME VOWS AS ARTEMIS. THEY WOULD NEVER MARRY, NEVER HAVE CHILDREN, NEVER KNOW THE TOUCH OF A MAN...
A SHAME, THAT, SO MANY BEAUTIFUL WOMEN... BUT I DIGRESS.

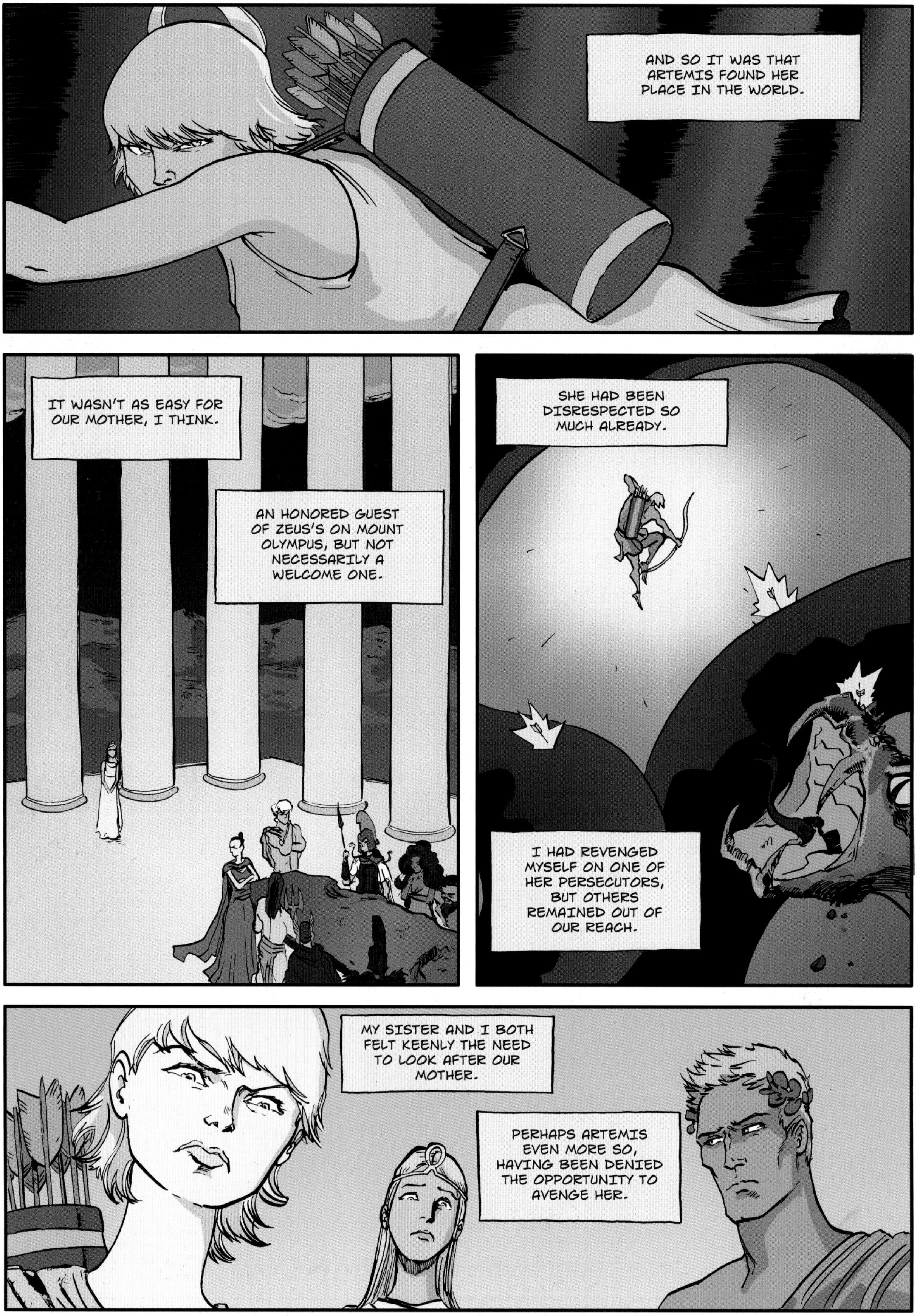
AND SO IT WAS THAT ARTEMIS FOUND HER PLACE IN THE WORLD.
IT WASN'T AS EASY FOR OUR MOTHER, I THINK.
AN HONORED GUEST OF ZEUS'S ON MOUNT OLYMPUS, BUT NOT NECESSARILY A WELCOME ONE.
SHE HAD BEEN DISRESPECTED SO MUCH ALREADY.
I HAD REVENGED MYSELF ON ONE OF HER PERSECUTORS, BUT OTHERS REMAINED OUT OF OUR REACH.
MY SISTER AND I BOTH FELT KEENLY THE NEED TO LOOK AFTER OUR MOTHER.
PERHAPS ARTEMIS EVEN MORE SO, HAVING BEEN DENIED THE OPPORTUNITY TO AVENGE HER.

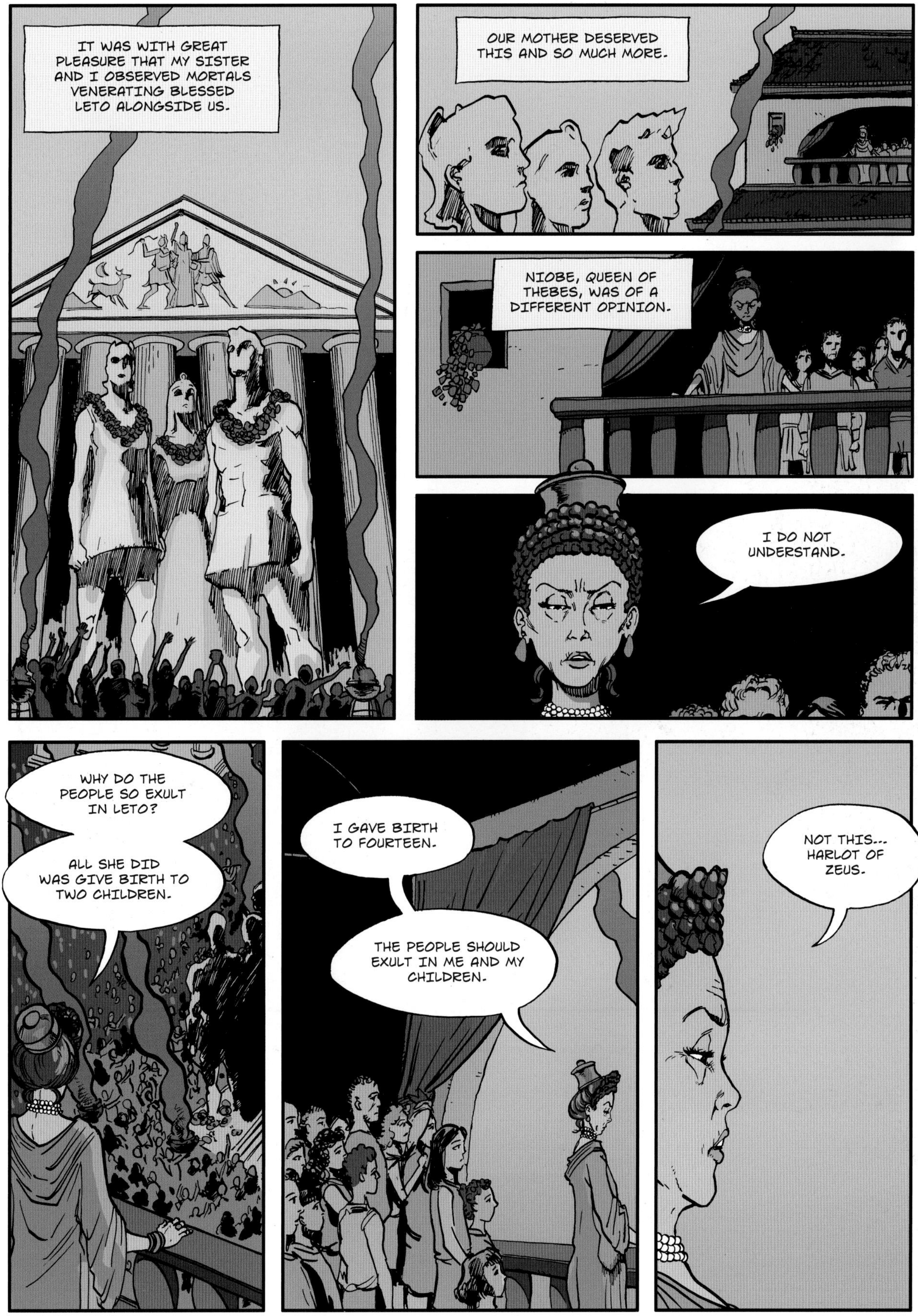

IT WAS WITH GREAT PLEASURE THAT MY SISTER AND I OBSERVED MORTALS VENERATING BLESSED LETO ALONGSIDE US.
OUR MOTHER DESERVED THIS AND SO MUCH MORE.
NIOBE, QUEEN OF THEBES, WAS OF A DIFFERENT OPINION.
I DO NOT UNDERSTAND.
WHY DO THE PEOPLE SO EXULT IN LETO?
ALL SHE DID WAS GIVE BIRTH TO TWO CHILDREN.
I GAVE BIRTH TO FOURTEEN.
THE PEOPLE SHOULD EXULT IN ME AND MY CHILDREN.
NOT THIS... HARLOT OF ZEUS.

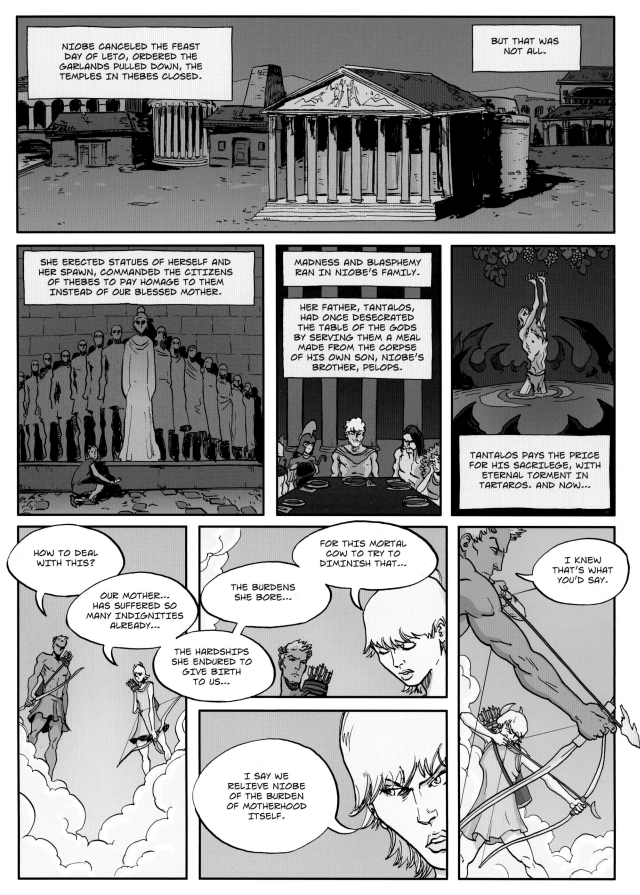

NIOBE CANCELED THE FEAST DAY OF LETO, ORDERED THE GARLANDS PULLED DOWN, THE TEMPLES IN THEBES CLOSED.

BUT THAT WAS NOT ALL.

SHE ERECTED STATUES OF HERSELF AND HER SPAWN, COMMANDED THE CITIZENS OF THEBES TO PAY HOMAGE TO THEM INSTEAD OF OUR BLESSED MOTHER.

MADNESS AND BLASPHEMY RAN IN NIOBE'S FAMILY.

HER FATHER, TANTALOS, HAD ONCE DESECRATED THE TABLE OF THE GODS BY SERVING THEM A MEAL MADE FROM THE CORPSE OF HIS OWN SON, NIOBE'S BROTHER, PELOPS.

TANTALOS PAYS THE PRICE FOR HIS SACRILEGE, WITH ETERNAL TORMENT IN TARTAROS. AND NOW...

HOW TO DEAL WITH THIS?

OUR MOTHER... HAS SUFFERED SO MANY INDIGNITIES ALREADY...

THE BURDENS SHE BORE...

THE HARDSHIPS SHE ENDURED TO GIVE BIRTH TO US...

FOR THIS MORTAL COW TO TRY TO DIMINISH THAT...

I KNEW THAT'S WHAT YOU'D SAY.

I SAY WE RELIEVE NIOBE OF THE BURDEN OF MOTHERHOOD ITSELF.

16

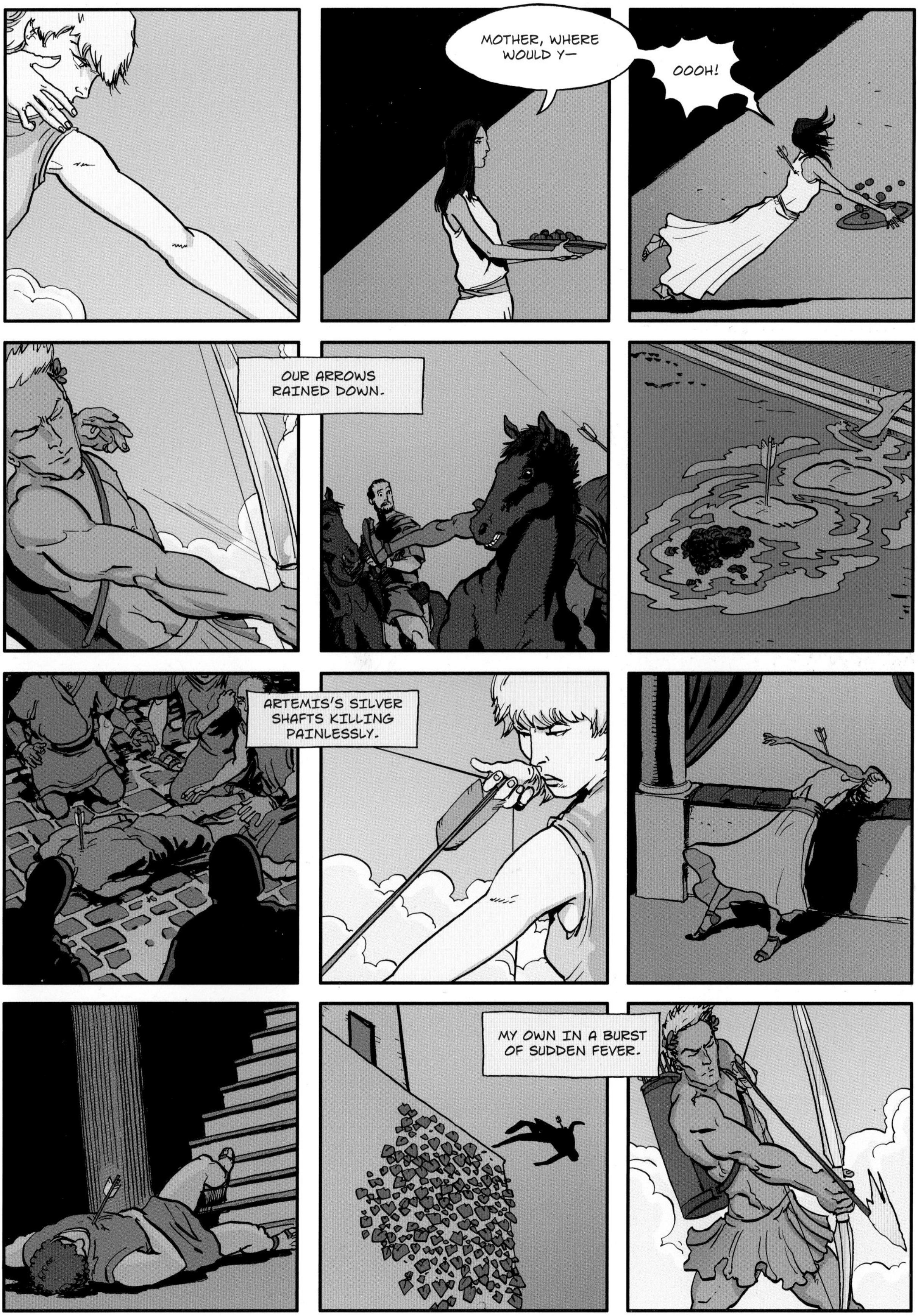
MOTHER, WHERE WOULD Y—
OOOH!
OUR ARROWS RAINED DOWN.
ARTEMIS'S SILVER SHAFTS KILLING PAINLESSLY.
MY OWN IN A BURST OF SUDDEN FEVER.

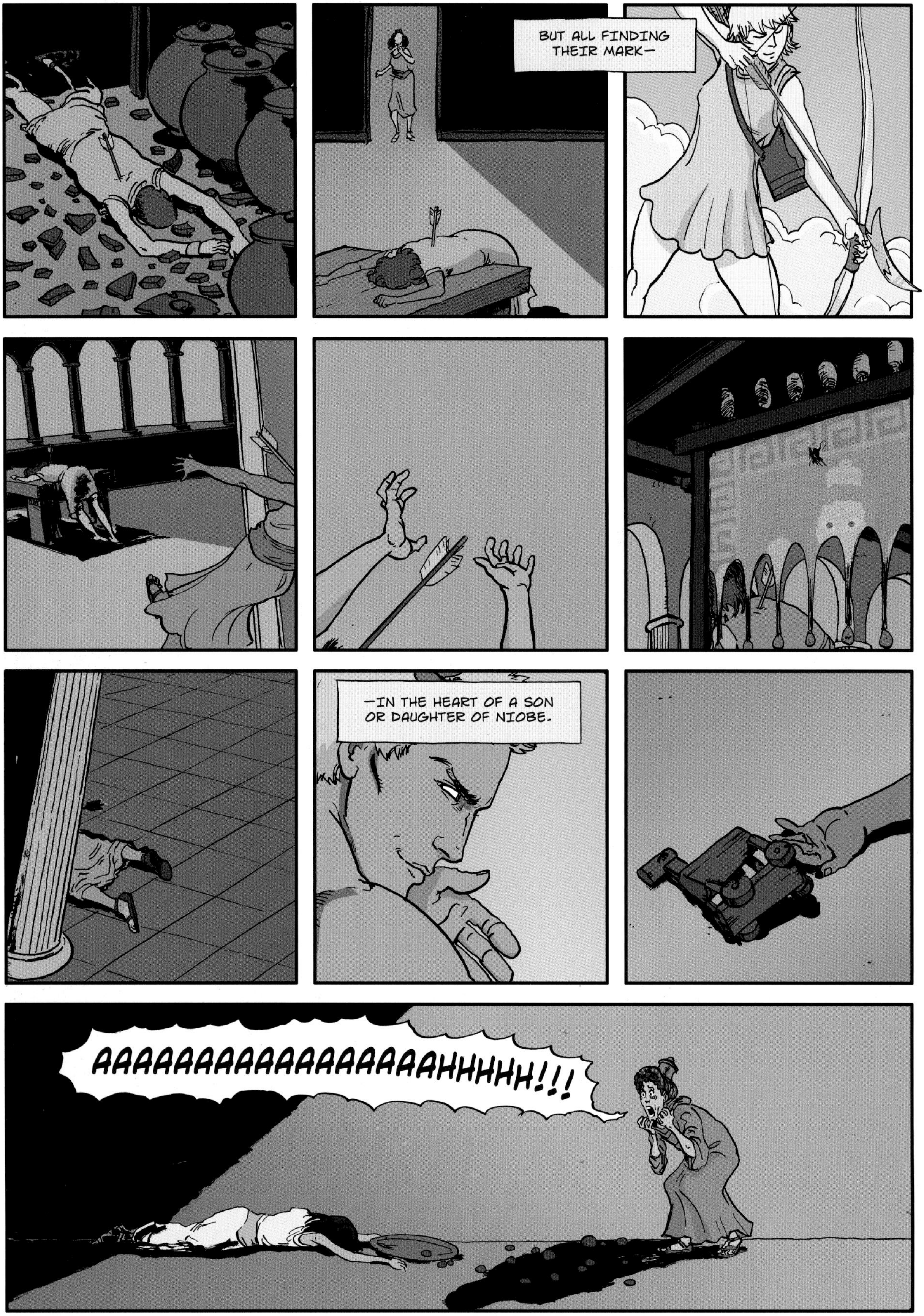
BUT ALL FINDING THEIR MARK—
—IN THE HEART OF A SON OR DAUGHTER OF NIOBE.
AAAAAAAAAAAAAAAAAAAHHHHH!!!

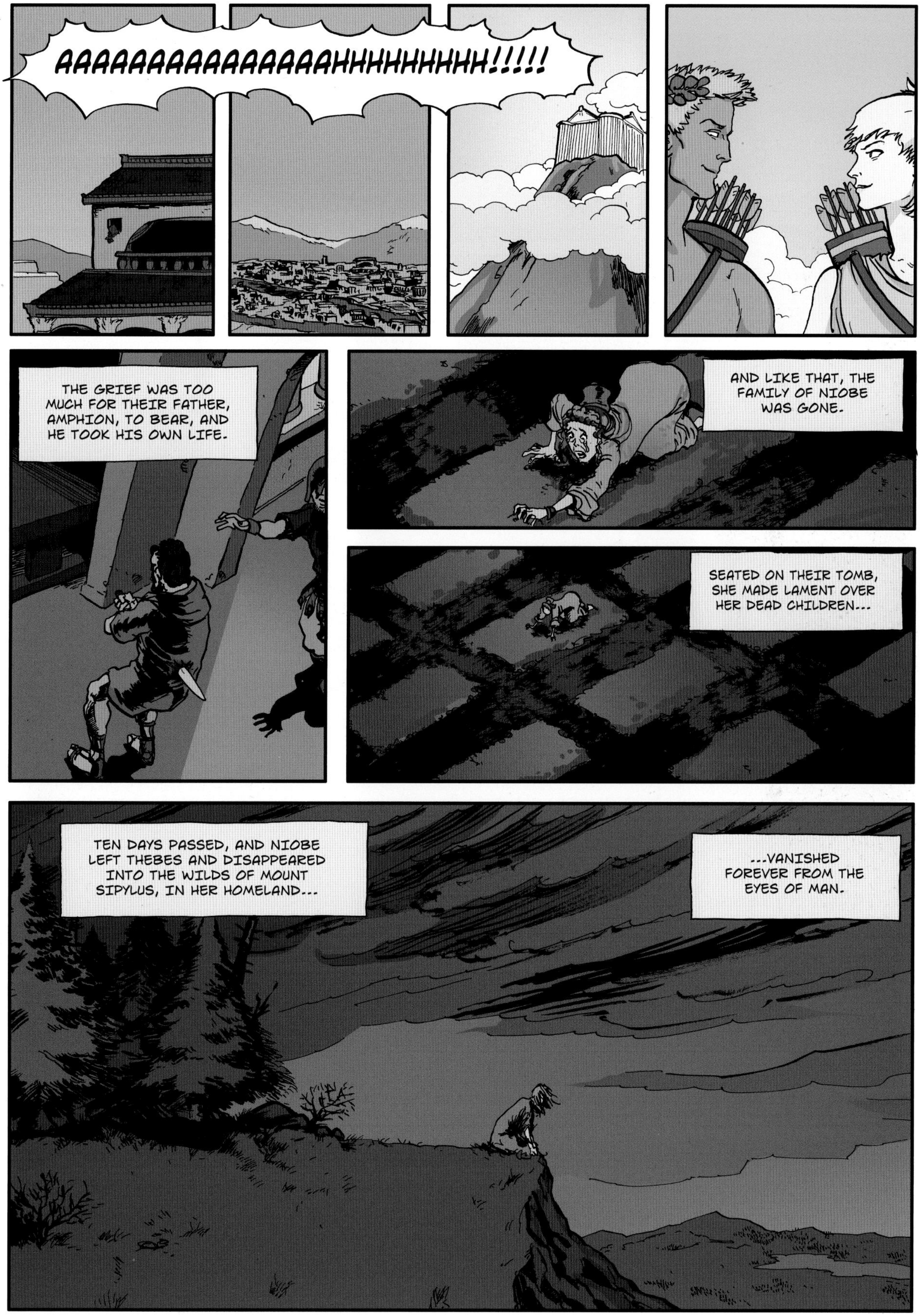
AAAAAAAAAAAAAAAAHHHHHHHHHH!!!!!
THE GRIEF WAS TOO MUCH FOR THEIR FATHER, AMPHION, TO BEAR, AND HE TOOK HIS OWN LIFE.
AND LIKE THAT, THE FAMILY OF NIOBE WAS GONE.
SEATED ON THEIR TOMB, SHE MADE LAMENT OVER HER DEAD CHILDREN...
TEN DAYS PASSED, AND NIOBE LEFT THEBES AND DISAPPEARED INTO THE WILDS OF MOUNT SIPYLUS, IN HER HOMELAND...
...VANISHED FOREVER FROM THE EYES OF MAN.

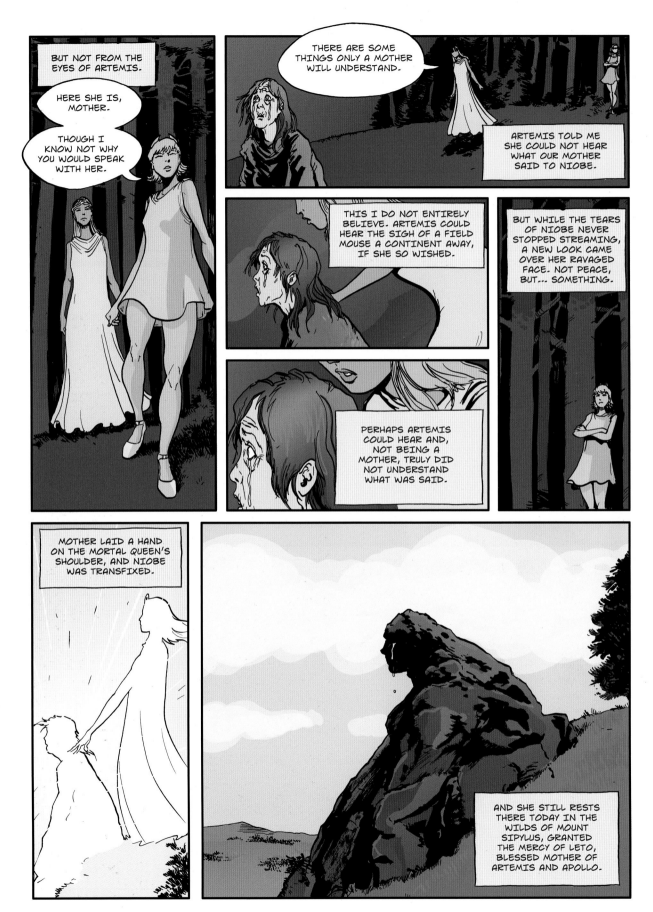

BUT NOT FROM THE EYES OF ARTEMIS.

HERE SHE IS, MOTHER.

THOUGH I KNOW NOT WHY YOU WOULD SPEAK WITH HER.

THERE ARE SOME THINGS ONLY A MOTHER WILL UNDERSTAND.

ARTEMIS TOLD ME SHE COULD NOT HEAR WHAT OUR MOTHER SAID TO NIOBE.

THIS I DO NOT ENTIRELY BELIEVE. ARTEMIS COULD HEAR THE SIGH OF A FIELD MOUSE A CONTINENT AWAY, IF SHE SO WISHED.

BUT WHILE THE TEARS OF NIOBE NEVER STOPPED STREAMING, A NEW LOOK CAME OVER HER RAVAGED FACE. NOT PEACE, BUT... SOMETHING.

PERHAPS ARTEMIS COULD HEAR AND, NOT BEING A MOTHER, TRULY DID NOT UNDERSTAND WHAT WAS SAID.

MOTHER LAID A HAND ON THE MORTAL QUEEN'S SHOULDER, AND NIOBE WAS TRANSFIXED.

AND SHE STILL RESTS THERE TODAY IN THE WILDS OF MOUNT SIPYLUS, GRANTED THE MERCY OF LETO, BLESSED MOTHER OF ARTEMIS AND APOLLO.

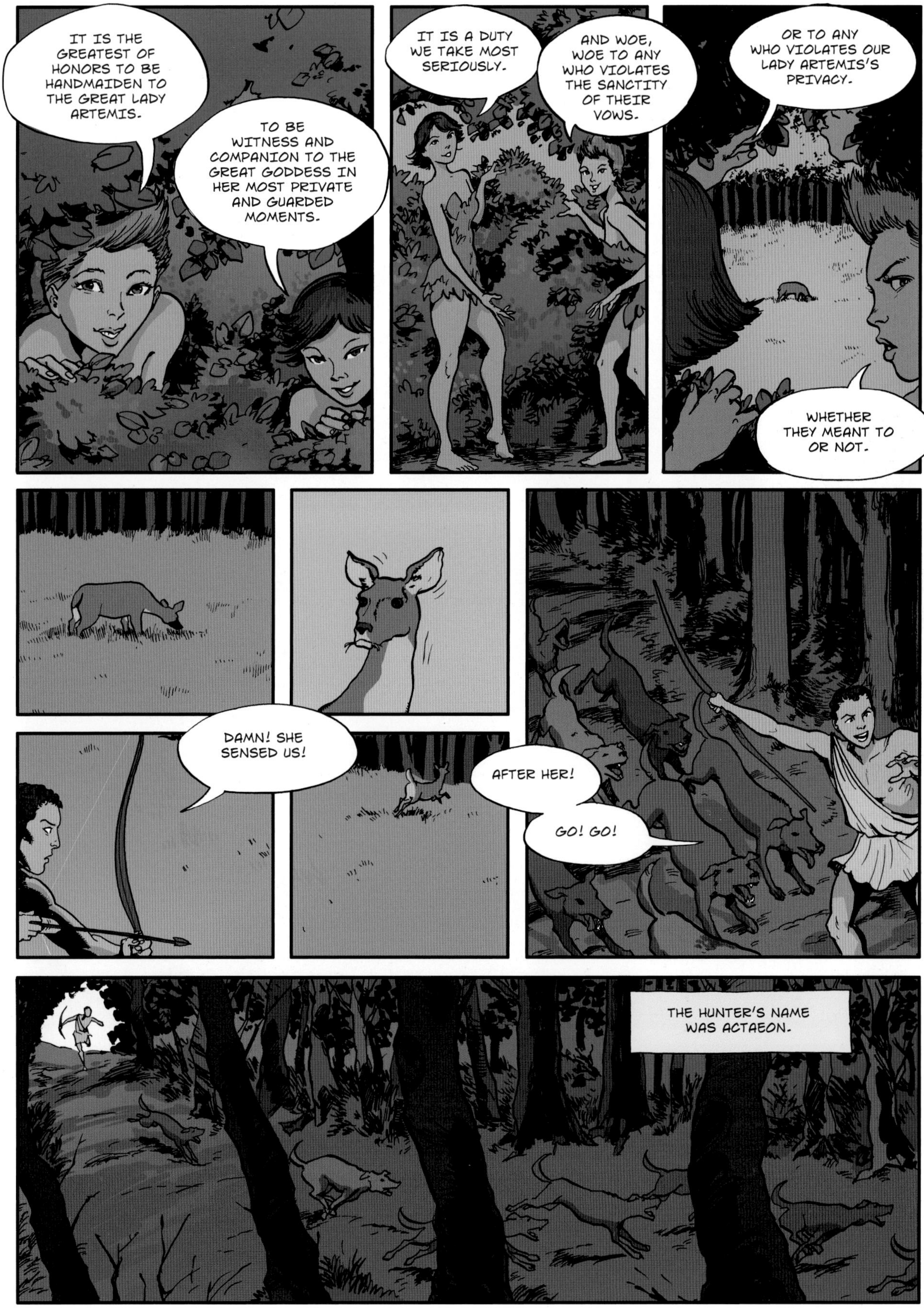
IT IS THE GREATEST OF HONORS TO BE HANDMAIDEN TO THE GREAT LADY ARTEMIS.
TO BE WITNESS AND COMPANION TO THE GREAT GODDESS IN HER MOST PRIVATE AND GUARDED MOMENTS.
IT IS A DUTY WE TAKE MOST SERIOUSLY.
AND WOE, WOE TO ANY WHO VIOLATES THE SANCTITY OF THEIR VOWS.
OR TO ANY WHO VIOLATES OUR LADY ARTEMIS'S PRIVACY.
WHETHER THEY MEANT TO OR NOT.
DAMN! SHE SENSED US!
AFTER HER!
GO! GO!
THE HUNTER'S NAME WAS ACTAEON.

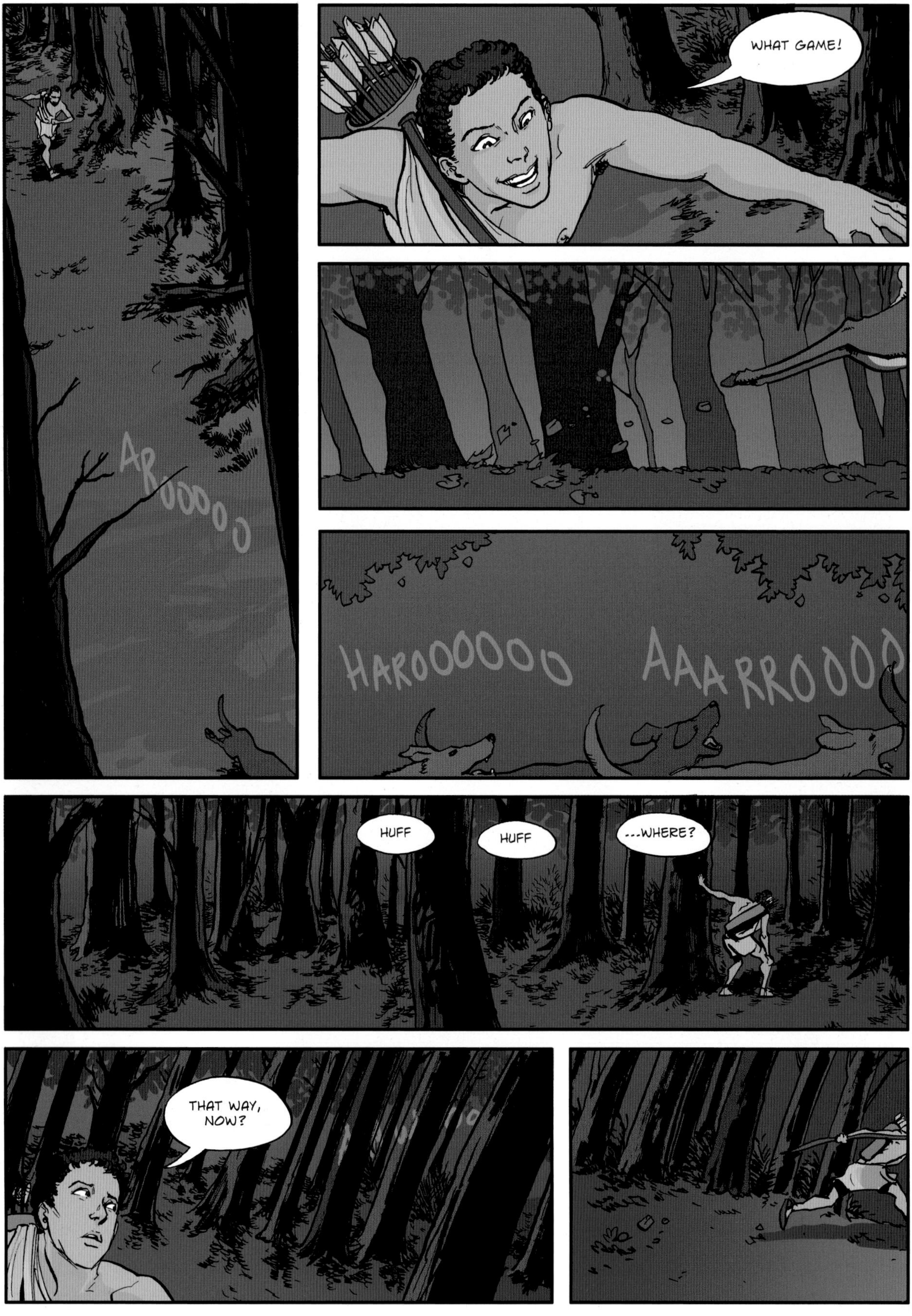
WHAT GAME!
AROOOOO
HAROOOOOO
AAARROOOO
HUFF
HUFF
...WHERE?
THAT WAY, NOW?

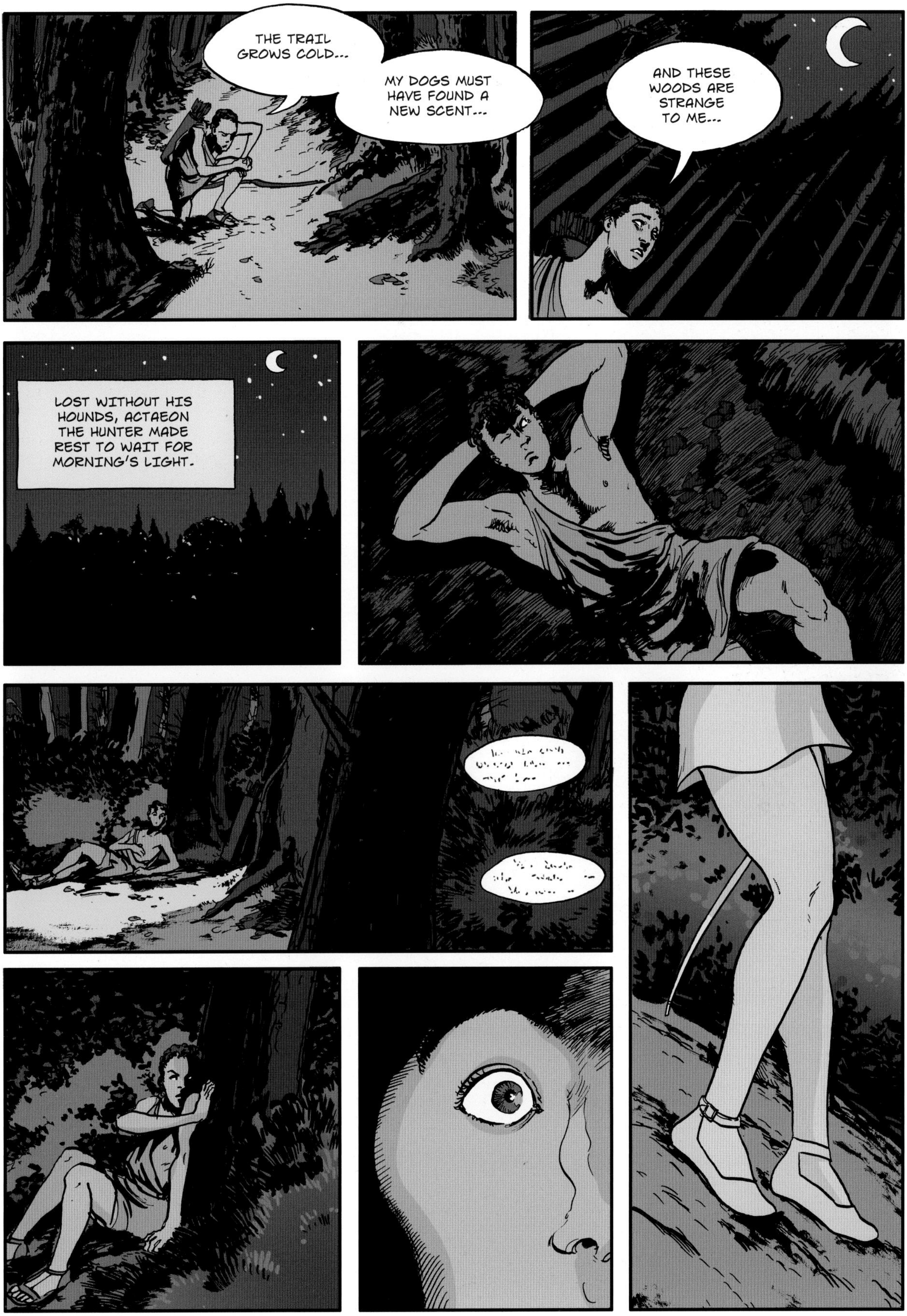
THE TRAIL GROWS COLD...
MY DOGS MUST HAVE FOUND A NEW SCENT...
AND THESE WOODS ARE STRANGE TO ME...
LOST WITHOUT HIS HOUNDS, ACTAEON THE HUNTER MADE REST TO WAIT FOR MORNING'S LIGHT.

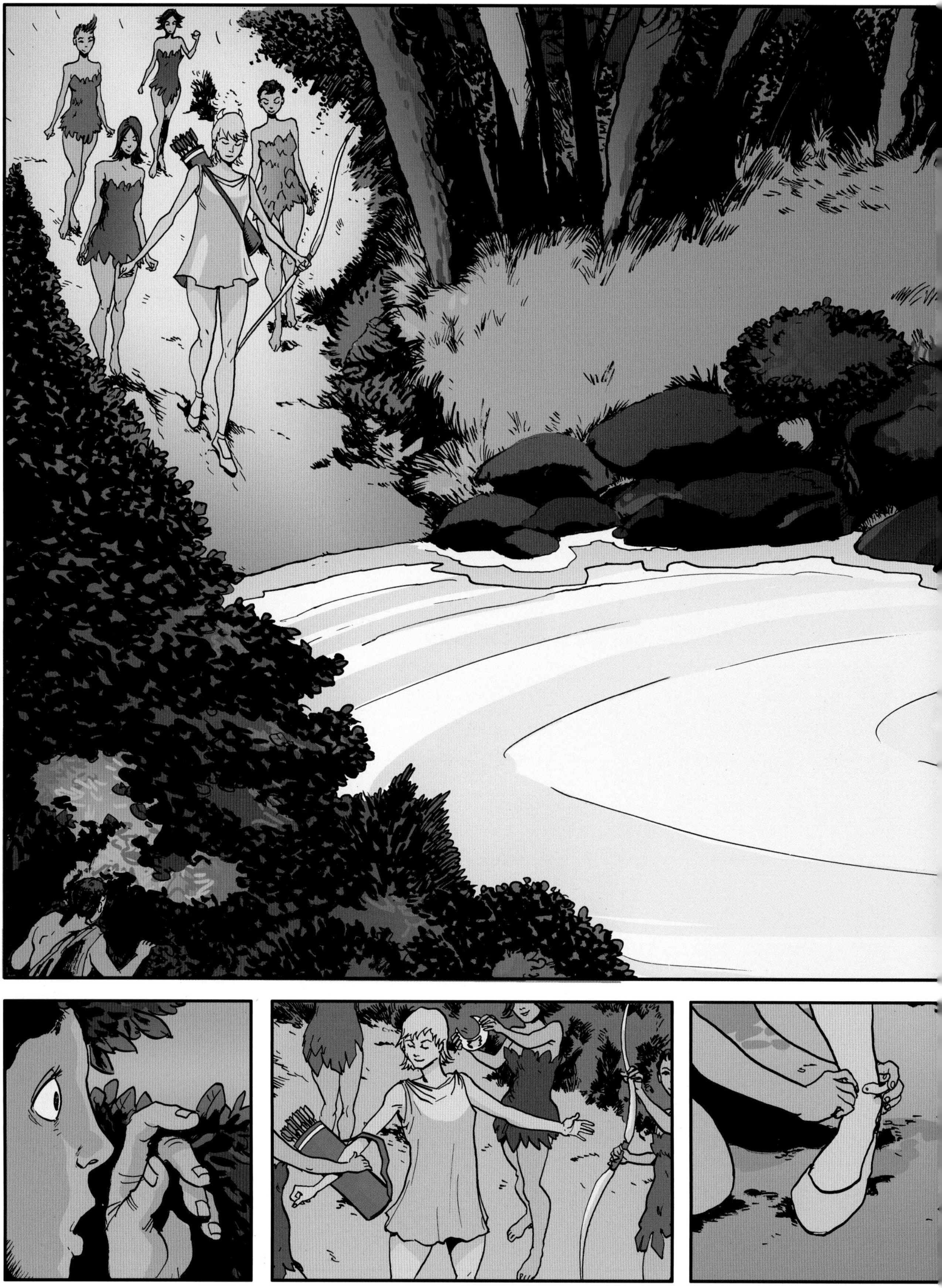

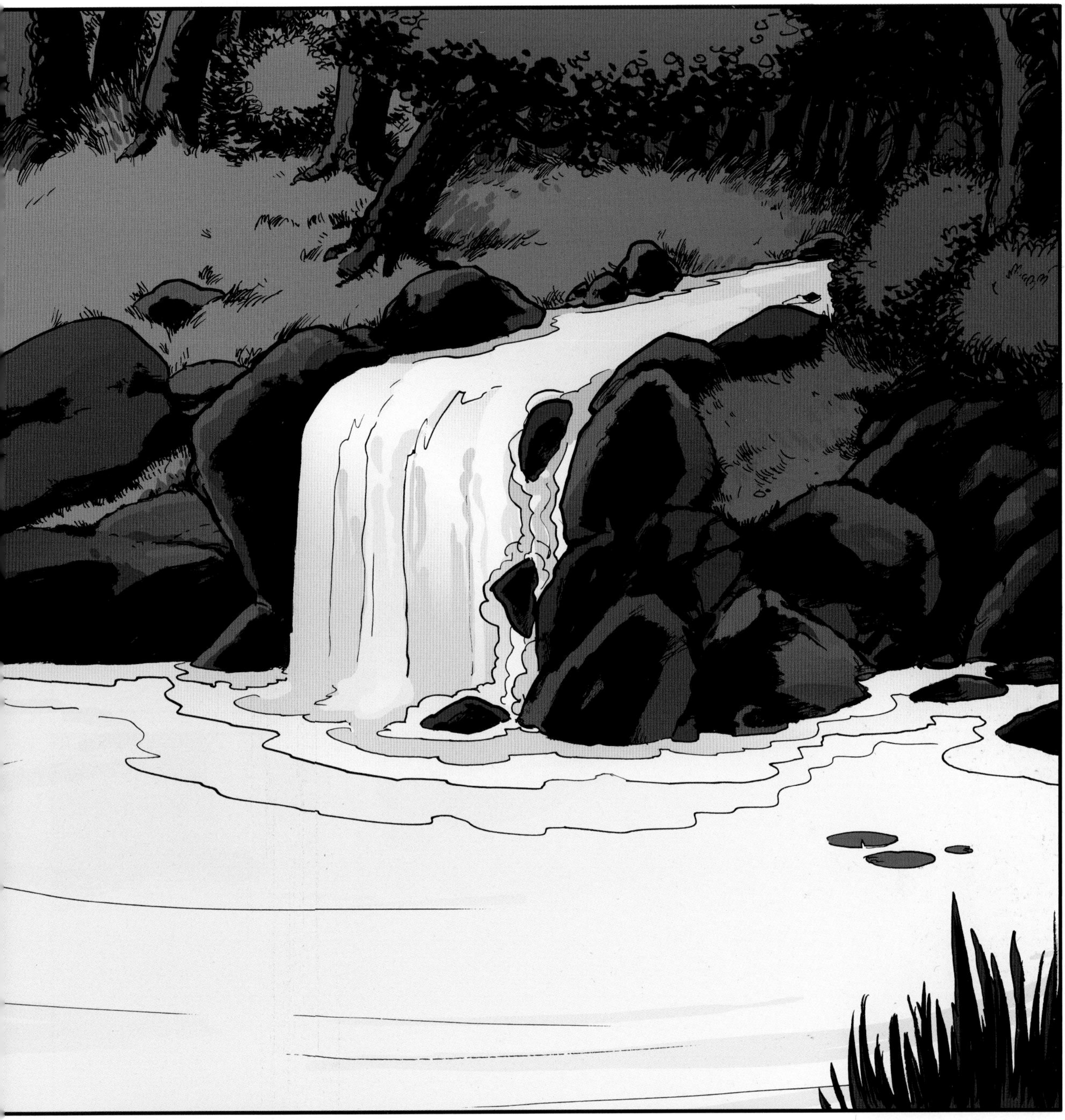

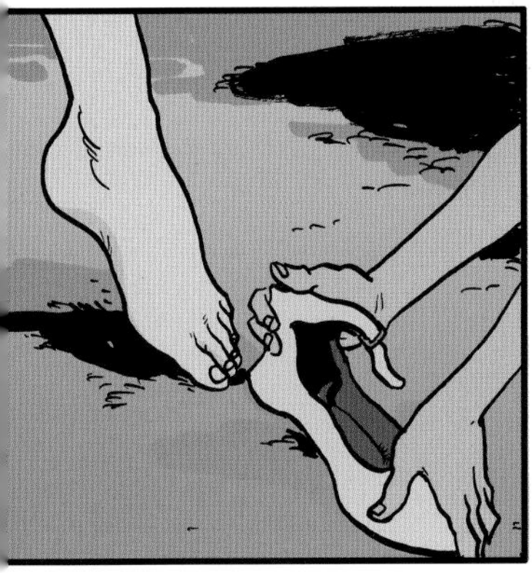

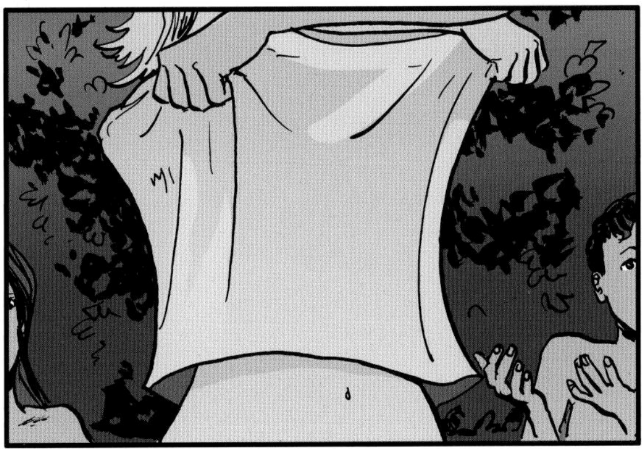

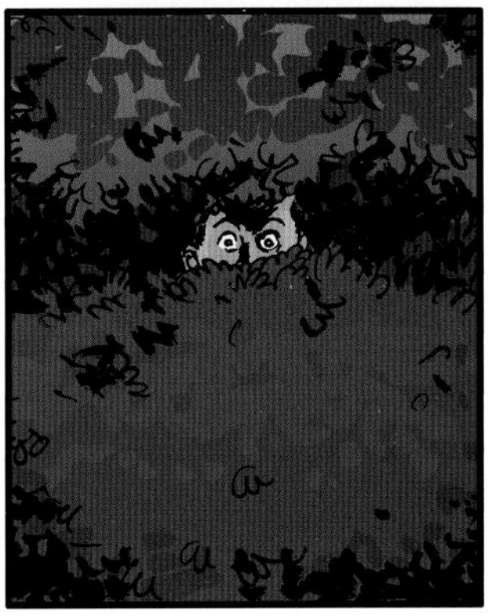

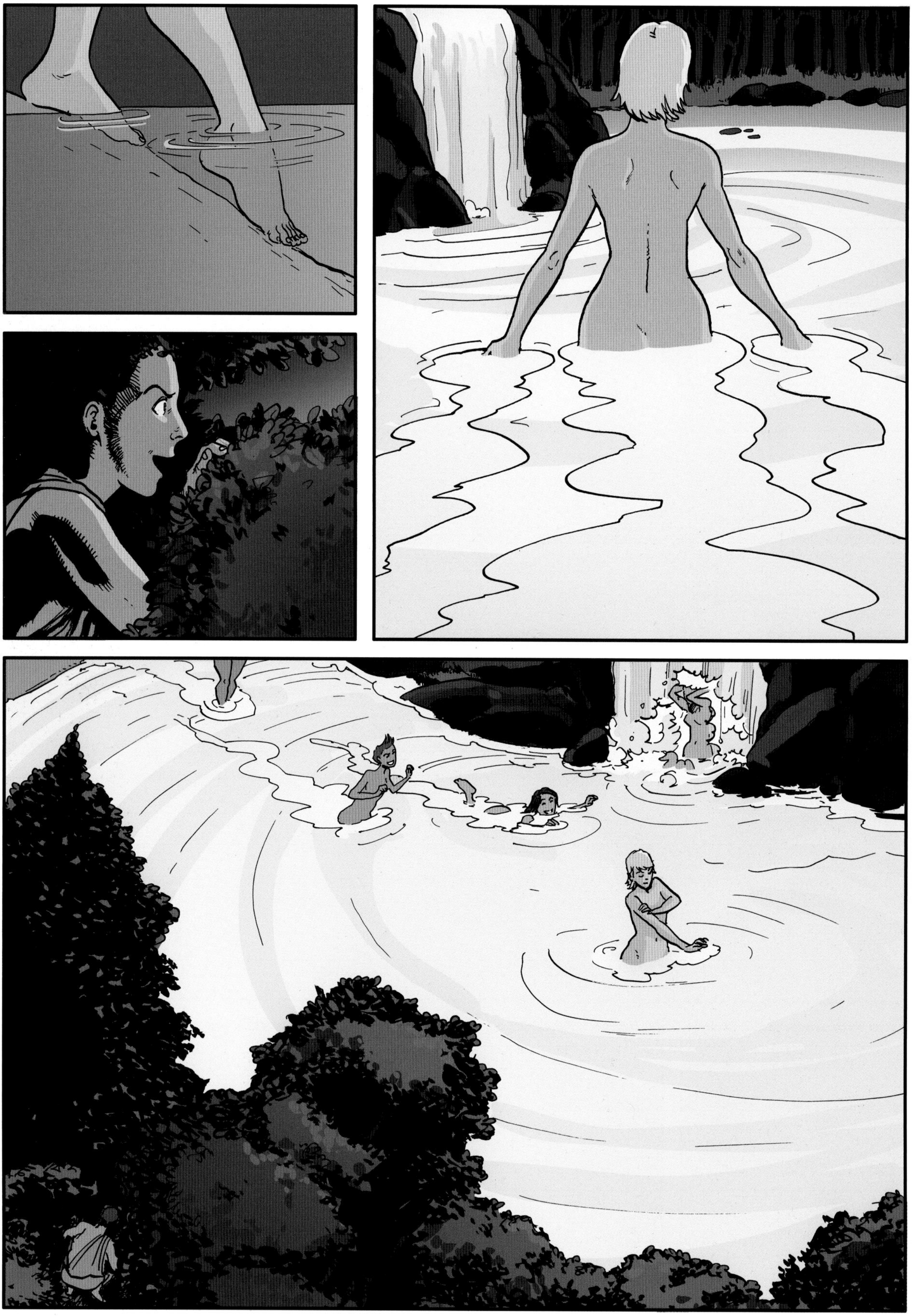

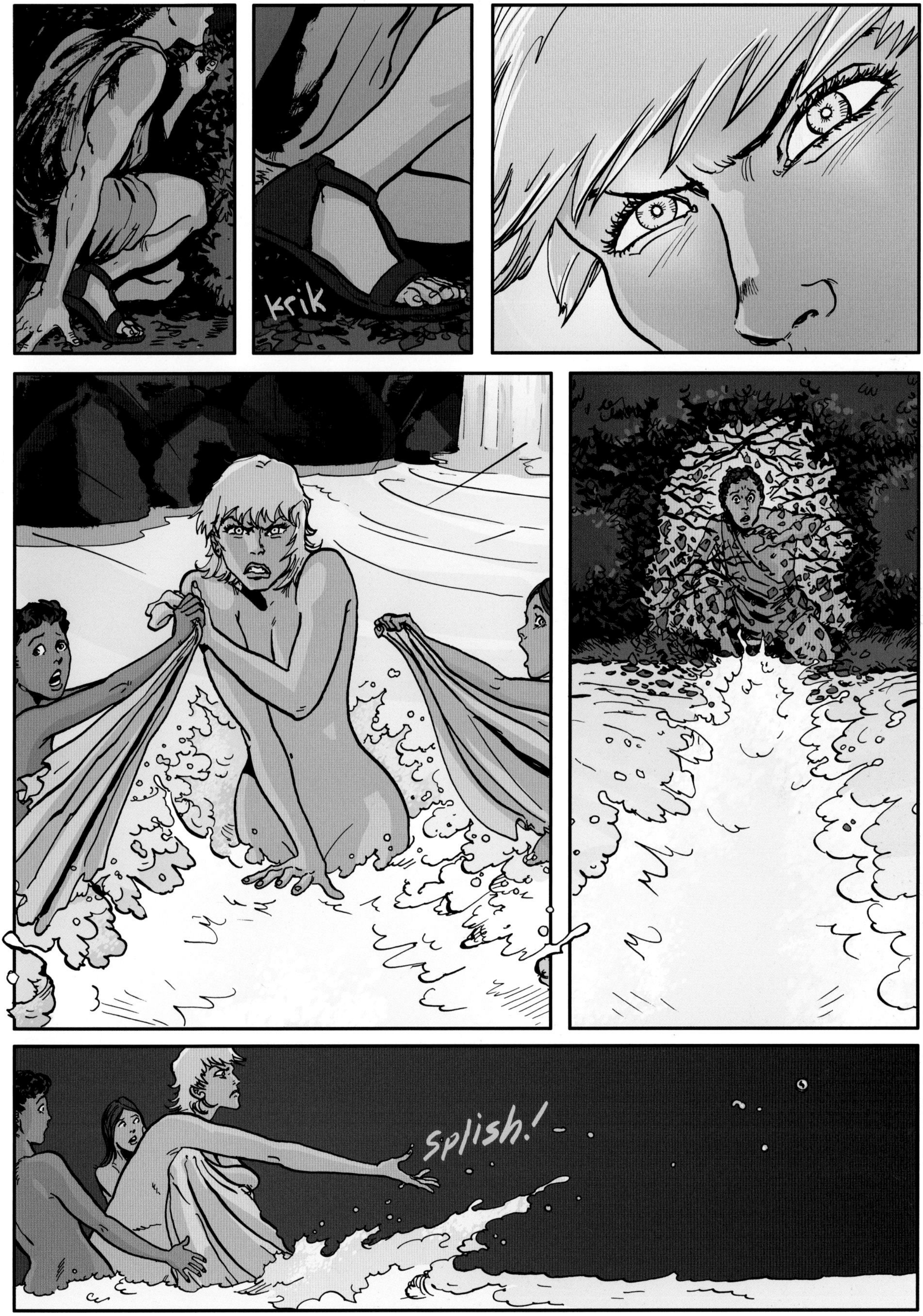
krik
splish!

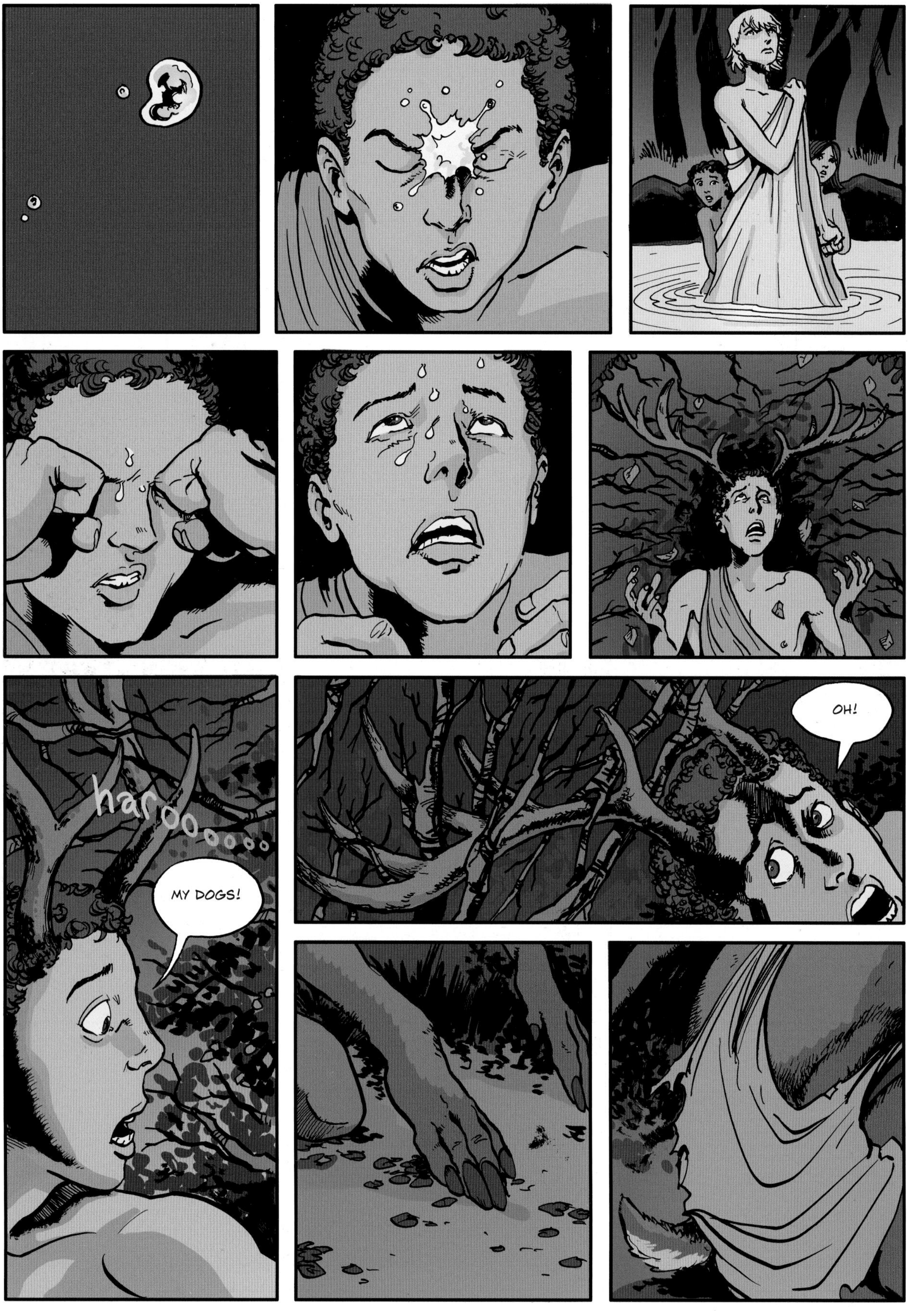
haroooooo
MY DOGS!
OH!

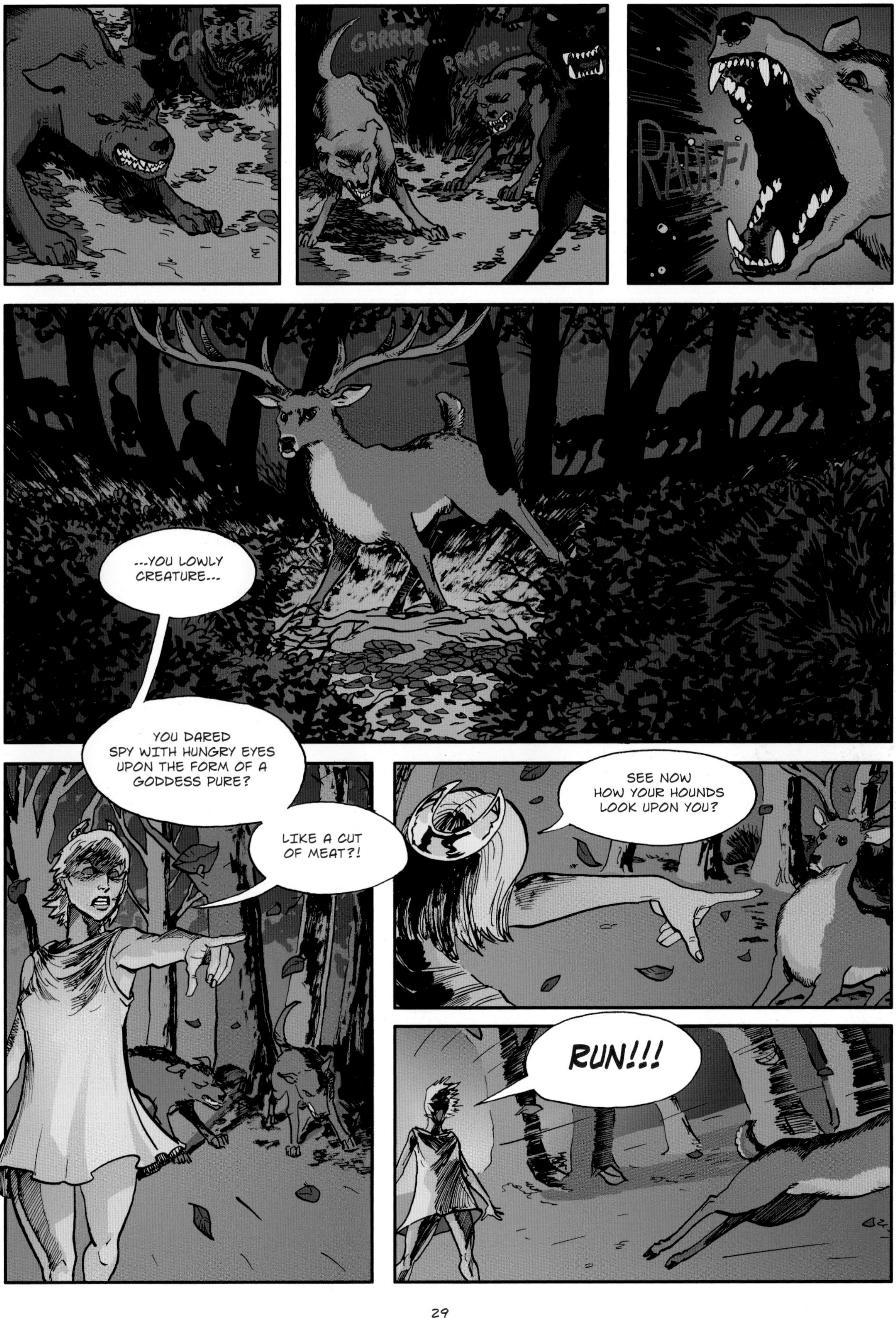
GRRRRR
GRRRRR...
RRRRR...
RAUFF!
...YOU LOWLY CREATURE...
YOU DARED SPY WITH HUNGRY EYES UPON THE FORM OF A GODDESS PURE?
LIKE A CUT OF MEAT?!
SEE NOW HOW YOUR HOUNDS LOOK UPON YOU?
RUN!!!

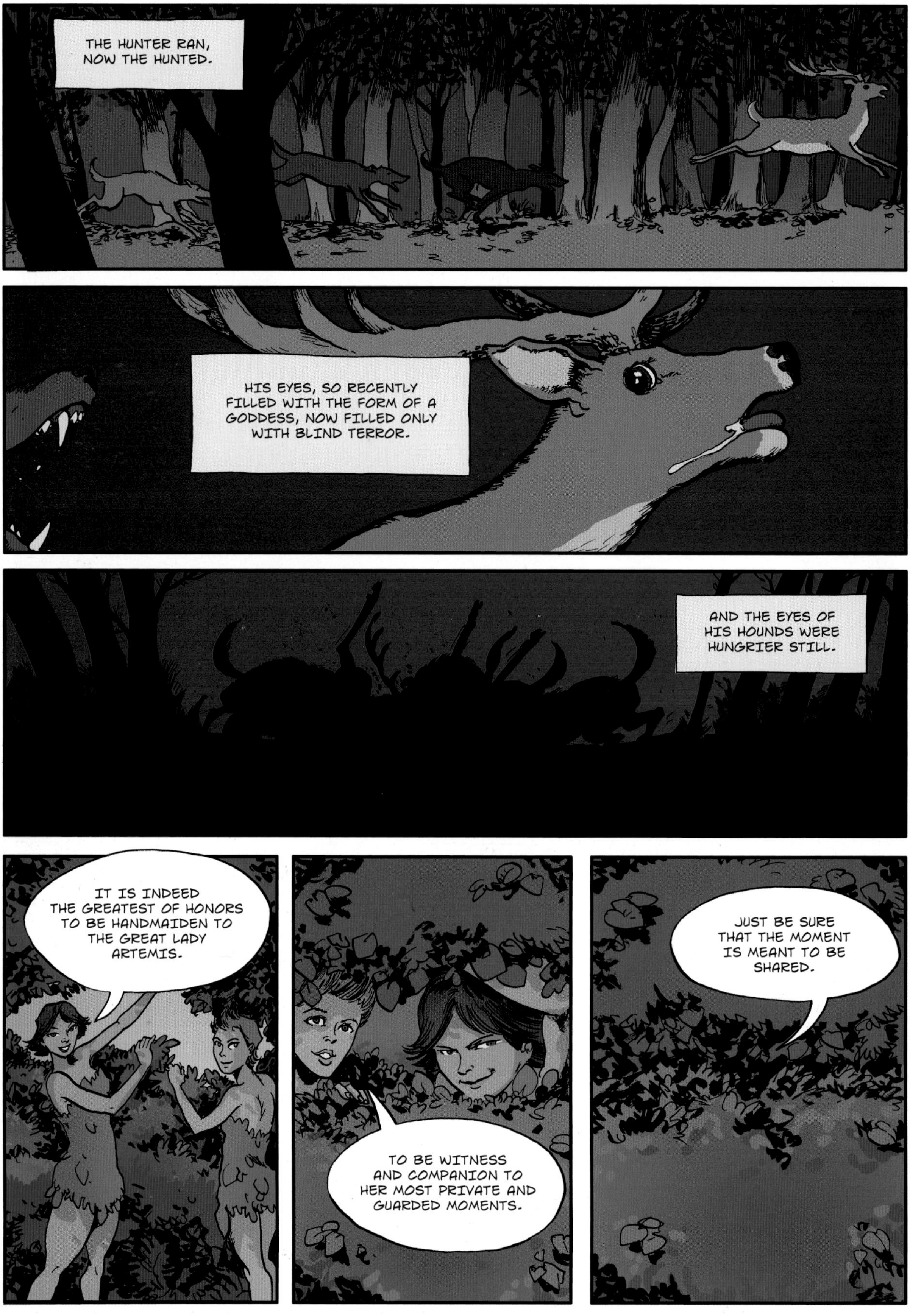
THE HUNTER RAN, NOW THE HUNTED.
HIS EYES, SO RECENTLY FILLED WITH THE FORM OF A GODDESS, NOW FILLED ONLY WITH BLIND TERROR.
AND THE EYES OF HIS HOUNDS WERE HUNGRIER STILL.
IT IS INDEED THE GREATEST OF HONORS TO BE HANDMAIDEN TO THE GREAT LADY ARTEMIS.
TO BE WITNESS AND COMPANION TO HER MOST PRIVATE AND GUARDED MOMENTS.
JUST BE SURE THAT THE MOMENT IS MEANT TO BE SHARED.

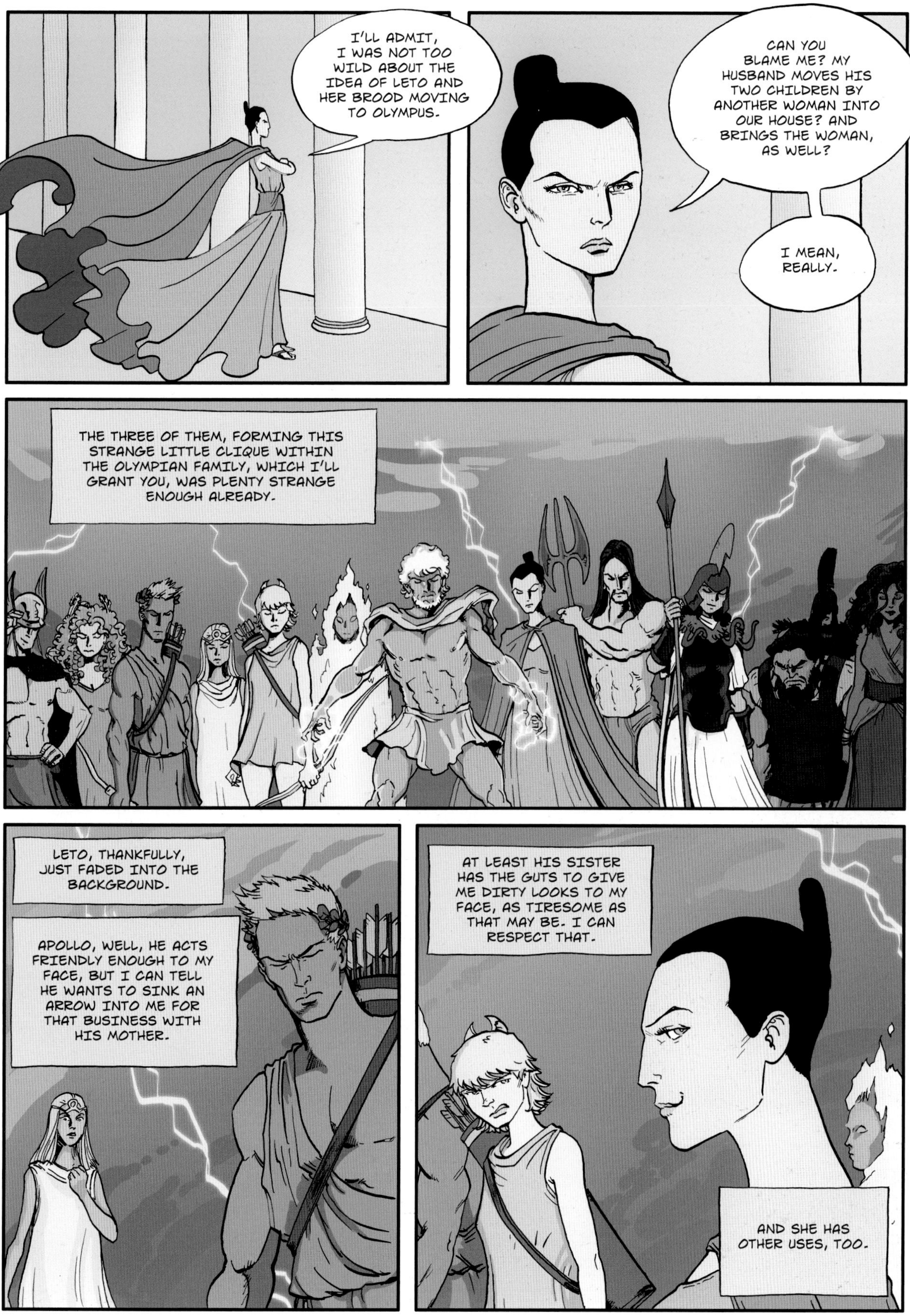
I'LL ADMIT, I WAS NOT TOO WILD ABOUT THE IDEA OF LETO AND HER BROOD MOVING TO OLYMPUS.
CAN YOU BLAME ME? MY HUSBAND MOVES HIS TWO CHILDREN BY ANOTHER WOMAN INTO OUR HOUSE? AND BRINGS THE WOMAN, AS WELL?
I MEAN, REALLY.
THE THREE OF THEM, FORMING THIS STRANGE LITTLE CLIQUE WITHIN THE OLYMPIAN FAMILY, WHICH I'LL GRANT YOU, WAS PLENTY STRANGE ENOUGH ALREADY.
LETO, THANKFULLY, JUST FADED INTO THE BACKGROUND.
APOLLO, WELL, HE ACTS FRIENDLY ENOUGH TO MY FACE, BUT I CAN TELL HE WANTS TO SINK AN ARROW INTO ME FOR THAT BUSINESS WITH HIS MOTHER.
AT LEAST HIS SISTER HAS THE GUTS TO GIVE ME DIRTY LOOKS TO MY FACE, AS TIRESOME AS THAT MAY BE. I CAN RESPECT THAT.
AND SHE HAS OTHER USES, TOO.

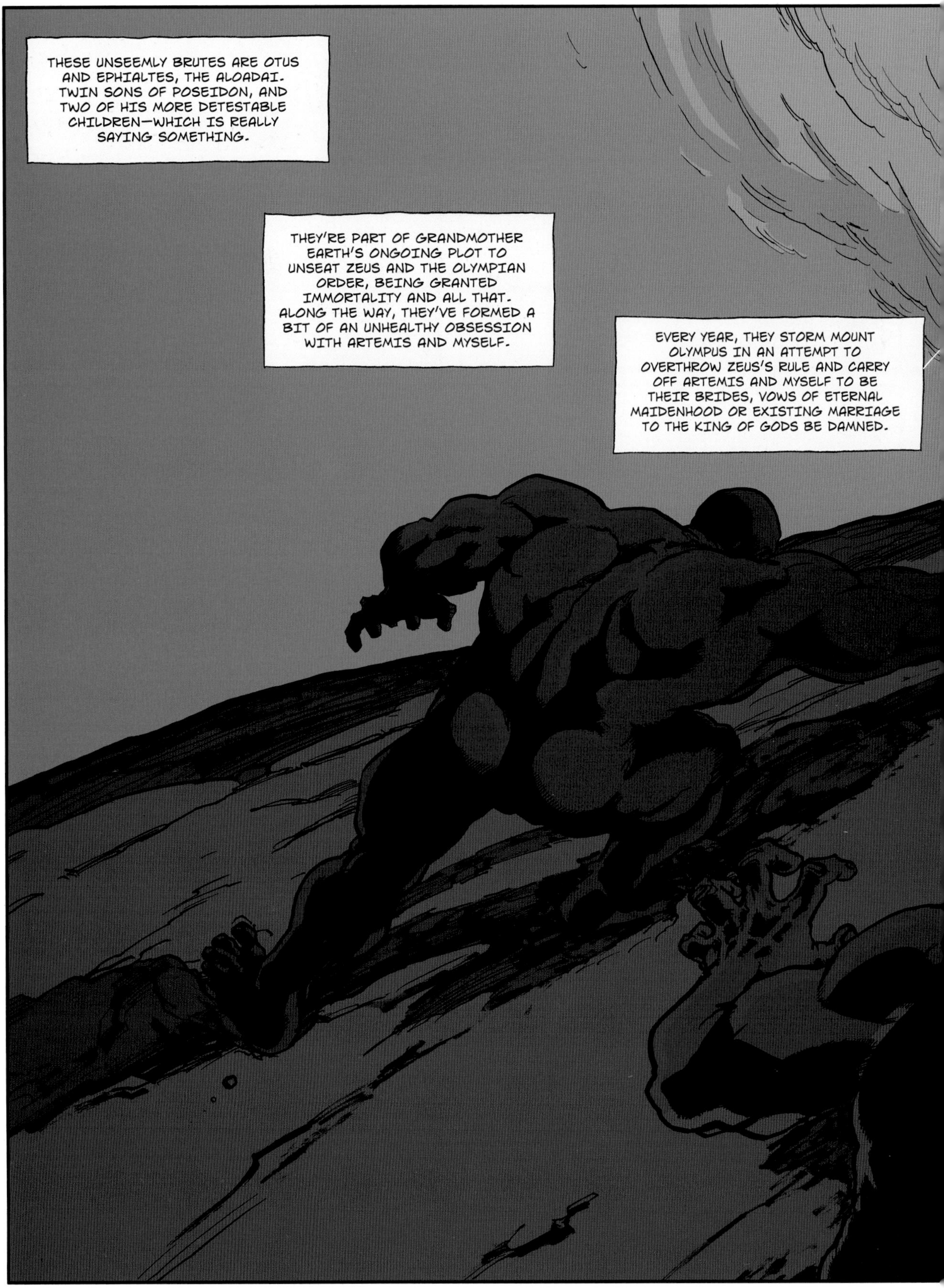
THESE UNSEEMLY BRUTES ARE OTUS AND EPHIALTES, THE ALOADAI. TWIN SONS OF POSEIDON, AND TWO OF HIS MORE DETESTABLE CHILDREN—WHICH IS REALLY SAYING SOMETHING.
THEY'RE PART OF GRANDMOTHER EARTH'S ONGOING PLOT TO UNSEAT ZEUS AND THE OLYMPIAN ORDER, BEING GRANTED IMMORTALITY AND ALL THAT. ALONG THE WAY, THEY'VE FORMED A BIT OF AN UNHEALTHY OBSESSION WITH ARTEMIS AND MYSELF.
EVERY YEAR, THEY STORM MOUNT OLYMPUS IN AN ATTEMPT TO OVERTHROW ZEUS'S RULE AND CARRY OFF ARTEMIS AND MYSELF TO BE THEIR BRIDES, VOWS OF ETERNAL MAIDENHOOD OR EXISTING MARRIAGE TO THE KING OF GODS BE DAMNED.

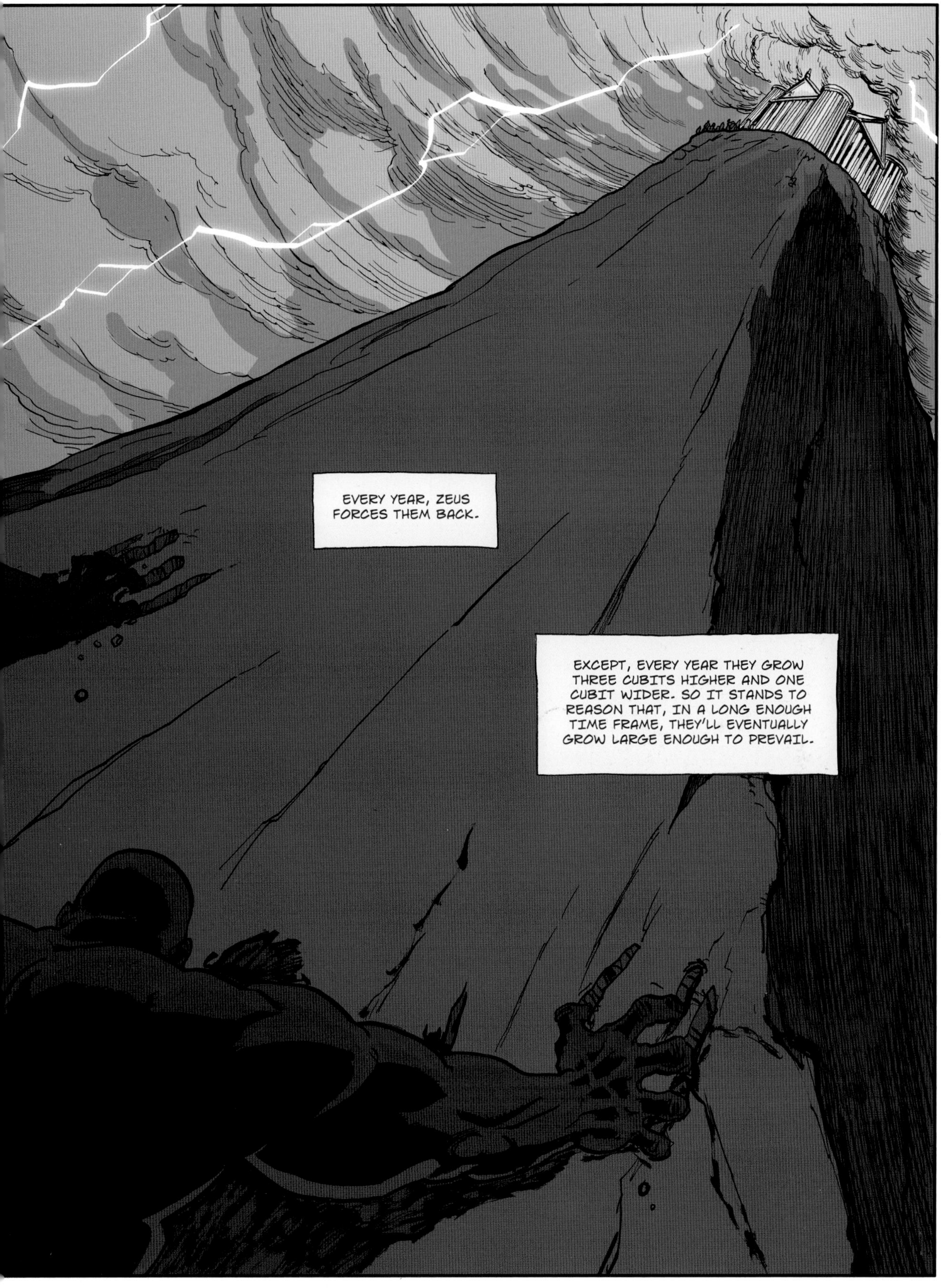
EVERY YEAR, ZEUS FORCES THEM BACK.
EXCEPT, EVERY YEAR THEY GROW THREE CUBITS HIGHER AND ONE CUBIT WIDER. SO IT STANDS TO REASON THAT, IN A LONG ENOUGH TIME FRAME, THEY'LL EVENTUALLY GROW LARGE ENOUGH TO PREVAIL.

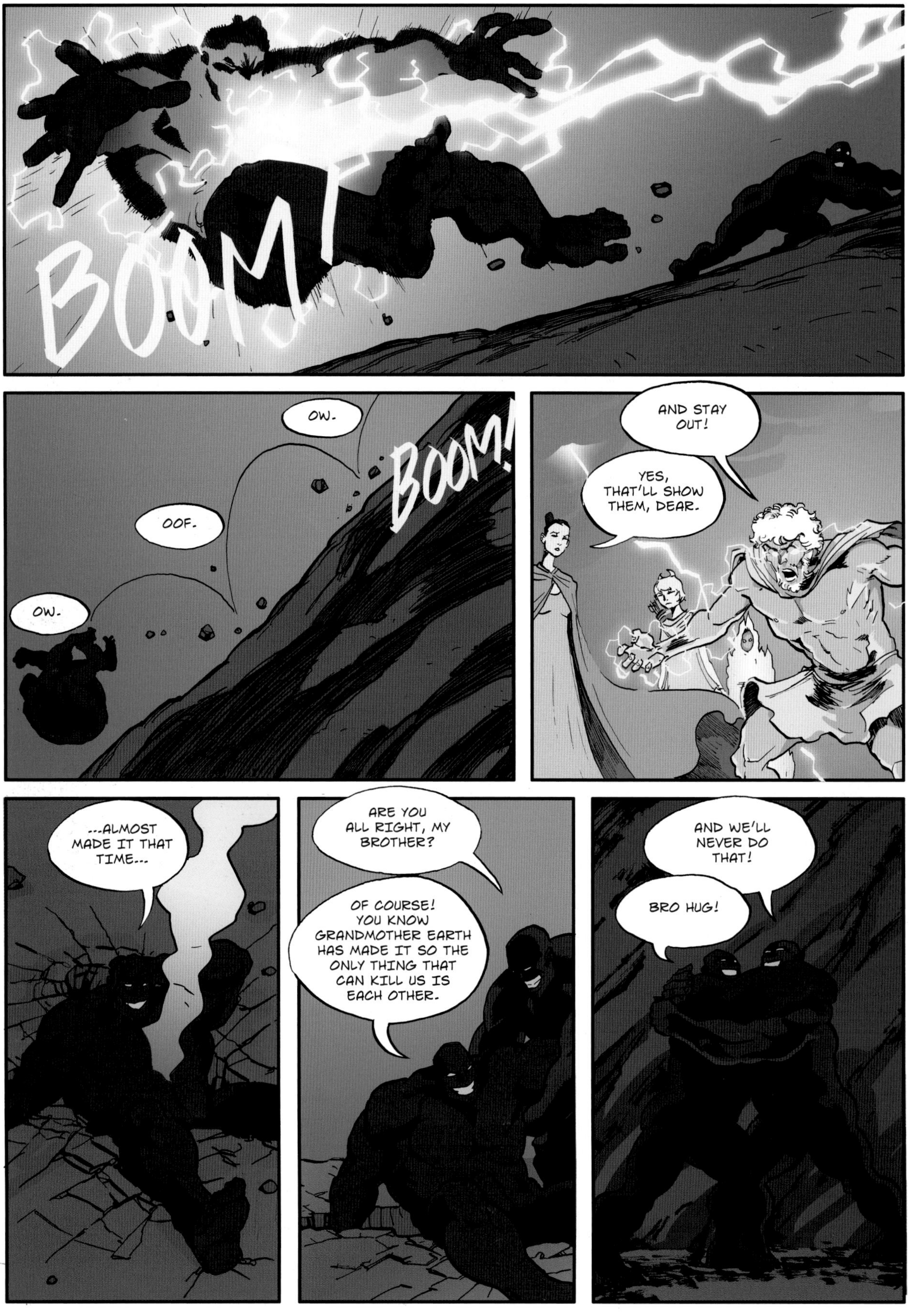
BOOM!
OW.
BOOM!
OOF.
OW.
AND STAY OUT!
YES, THAT'LL SHOW THEM, DEAR.
...ALMOST MADE IT THAT TIME...
ARE YOU ALL RIGHT, MY BROTHER?
OF COURSE! YOU KNOW GRANDMOTHER EARTH HAS MADE IT SO THE ONLY THING THAT CAN KILL US IS EACH OTHER.
AND WE'LL NEVER DO THAT!
BRO HUG!

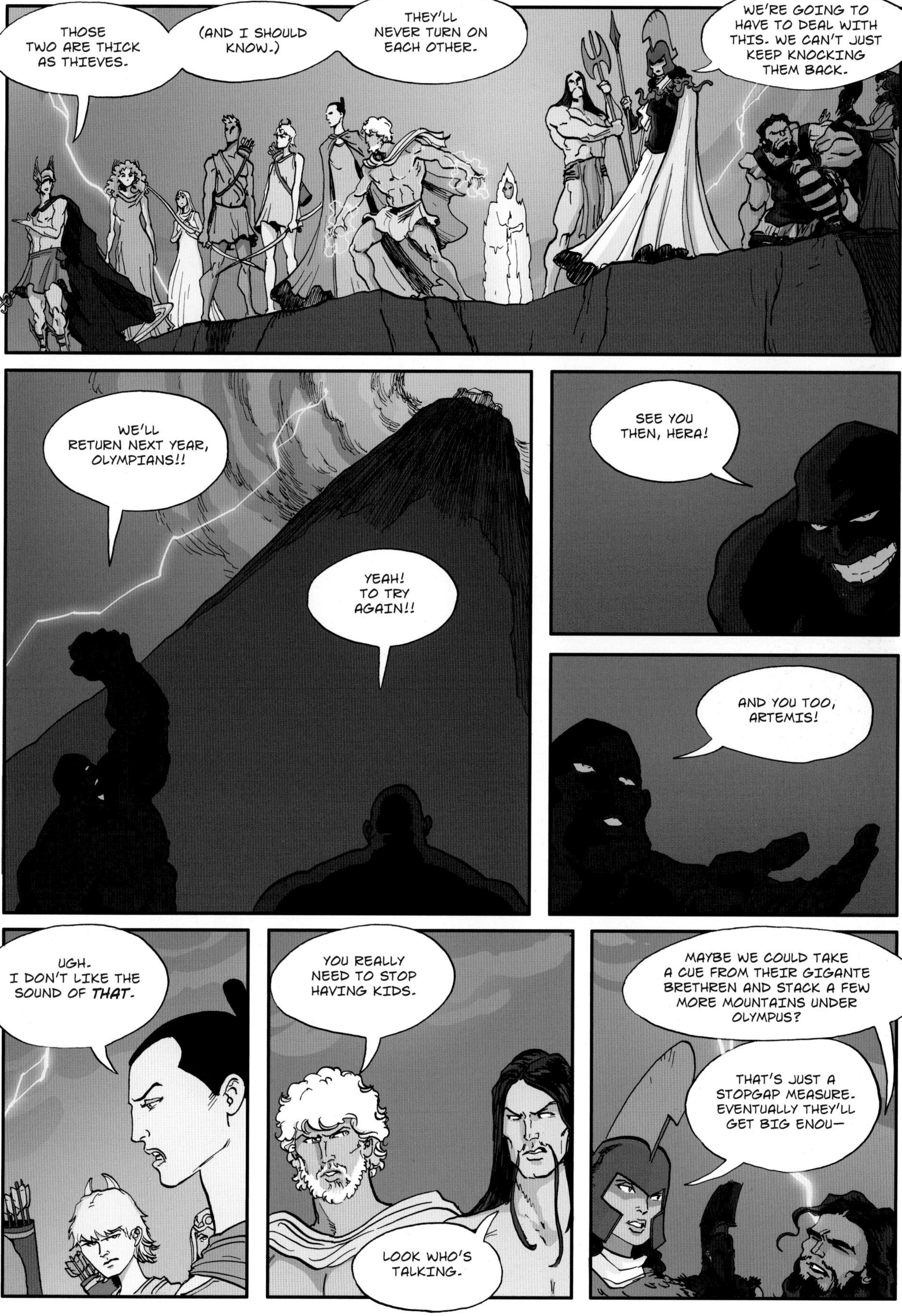
THOSE TWO ARE THICK AS THIEVES.
(AND I SHOULD KNOW.)
THEY'LL NEVER TURN ON EACH OTHER.
WE'RE GOING TO HAVE TO DEAL WITH THIS. WE CAN'T JUST KEEP KNOCKING THEM BACK.
WE'LL RETURN NEXT YEAR, OLYMPIANS!!
YEAH! TO TRY AGAIN!!
SEE YOU THEN, HERA!
AND YOU TOO, ARTEMIS!
UGH. I DON'T LIKE THE SOUND OF *THAT*.
YOU REALLY NEED TO STOP HAVING KIDS.
LOOK WHO'S TALKING.
MAYBE WE COULD TAKE A CUE FROM THEIR GIGANTE BRETHREN AND STACK A FEW MORE MOUNTAINS UNDER OLYMPUS?
THAT'S JUST A STOPGAP MEASURE. EVENTUALLY THEY'LL GET BIG ENOU—

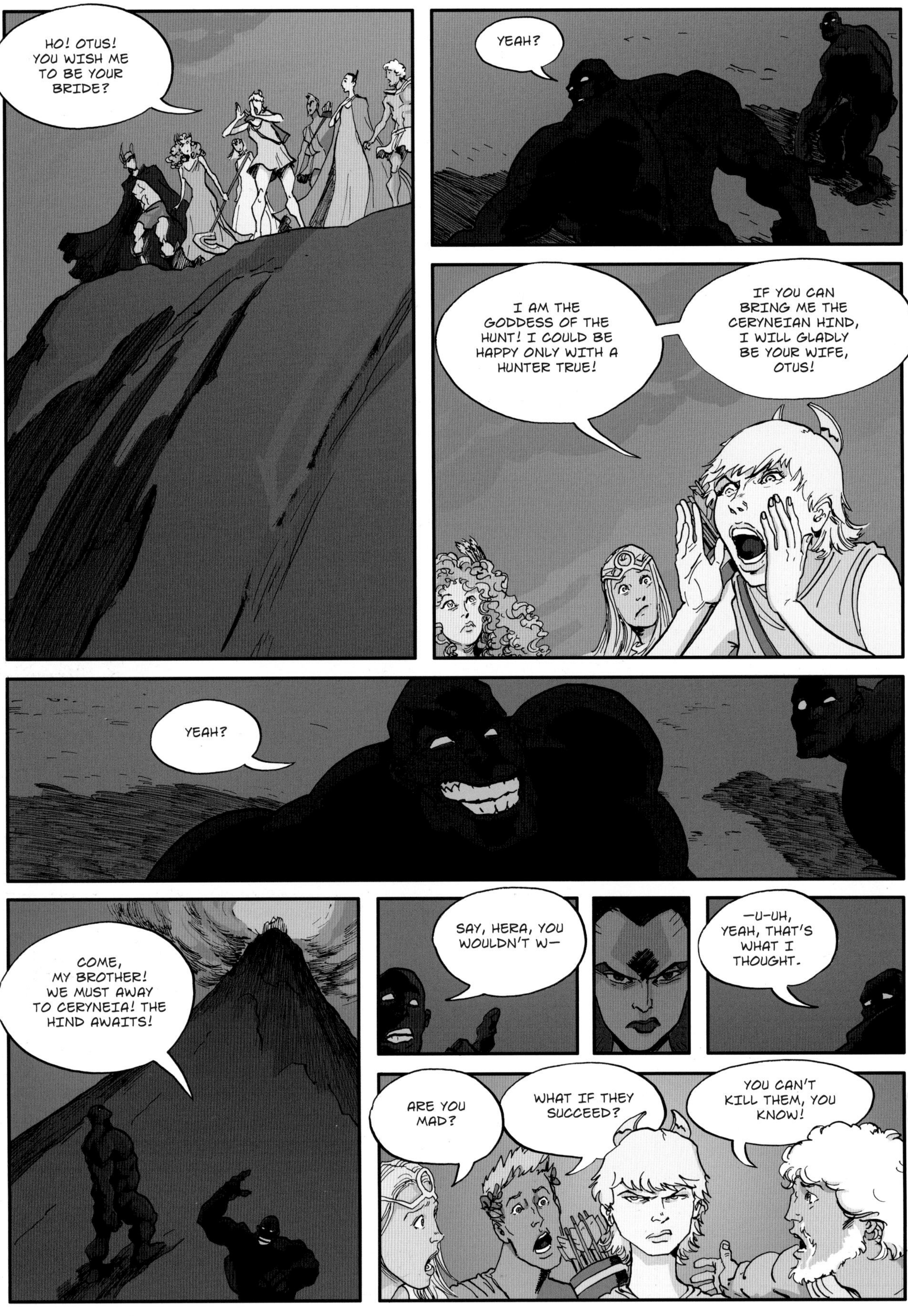
HO! OTUS! YOU WISH ME TO BE YOUR BRIDE?
YEAH?
I AM THE GODDESS OF THE HUNT! I COULD BE HAPPY ONLY WITH A HUNTER TRUE!
IF YOU CAN BRING ME THE CERYNEIAN HIND, I WILL GLADLY BE YOUR WIFE, OTUS!
YEAH?
COME, MY BROTHER! WE MUST AWAY TO CERYNEIA! THE HIND AWAITS!
SAY, HERA, YOU WOULDN'T W—
—U-UH, YEAH, THAT'S WHAT I THOUGHT.
ARE YOU MAD?
WHAT IF THEY SUCCEED?
YOU CAN'T KILL THEM, YOU KNOW!

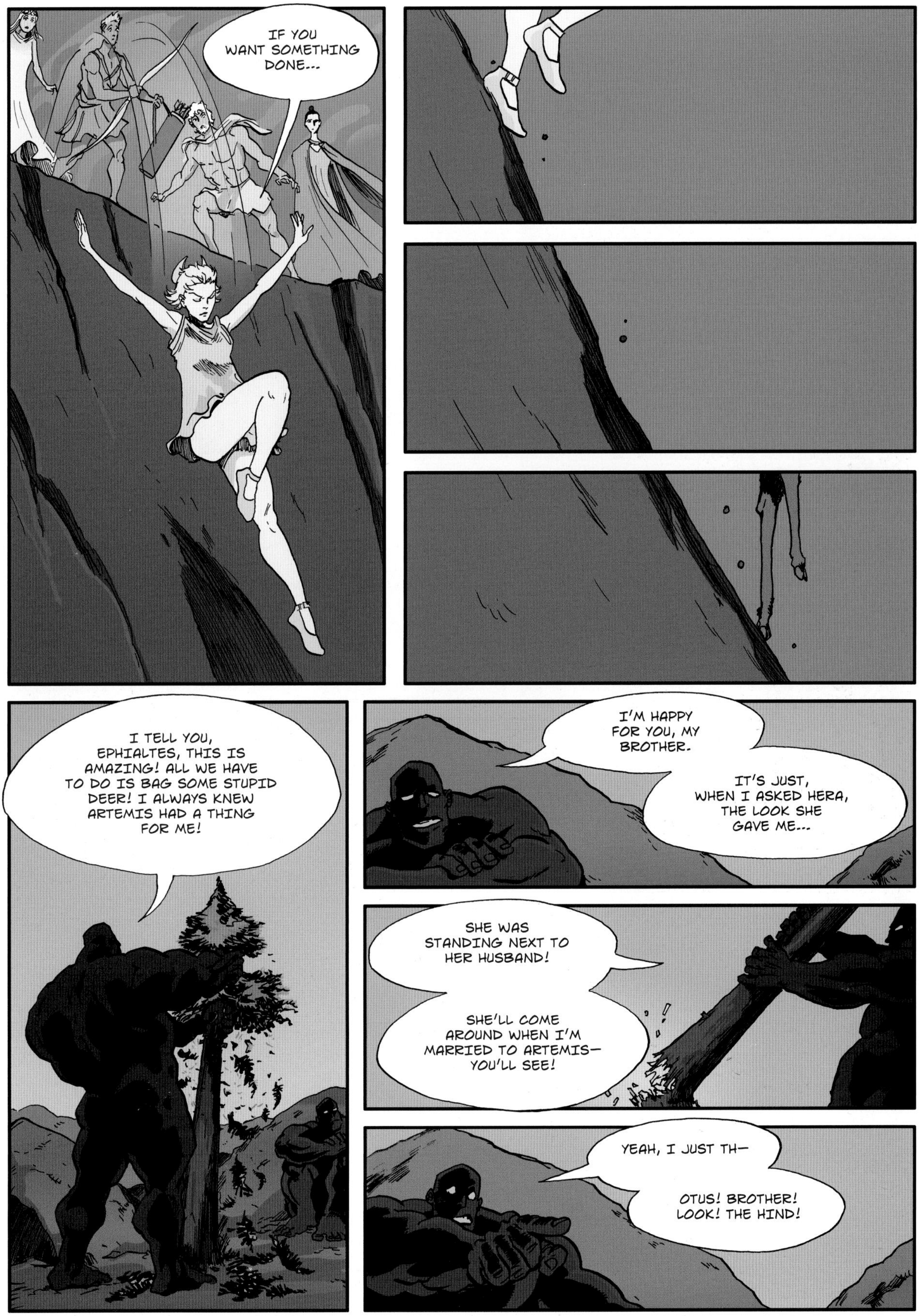
IF YOU WANT SOMETHING DONE...
I TELL YOU, EPHIALTES, THIS IS AMAZING! ALL WE HAVE TO DO IS BAG SOME STUPID DEER! I ALWAYS KNEW ARTEMIS HAD A THING FOR ME!
I'M HAPPY FOR YOU, MY BROTHER.
IT'S JUST, WHEN I ASKED HERA, THE LOOK SHE GAVE ME...
SHE WAS STANDING NEXT TO HER HUSBAND!
SHE'LL COME AROUND WHEN I'M MARRIED TO ARTEMIS—YOU'LL SEE!
YEAH, I JUST TH—
OTUS! BROTHER! LOOK! THE HIND!

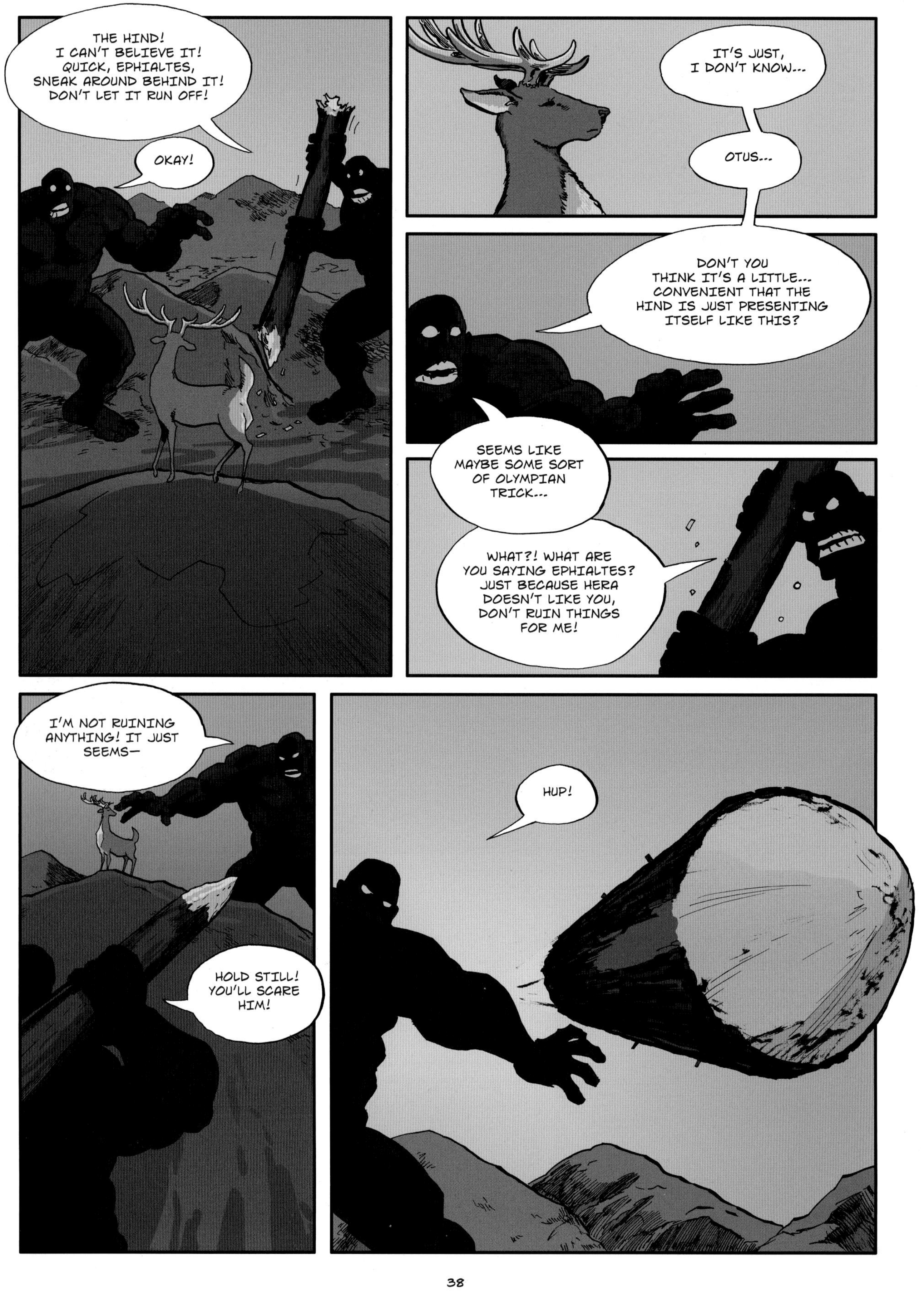
THE HIND! I CAN'T BELIEVE IT! QUICK, EPHIALTES, SNEAK AROUND BEHIND IT! DON'T LET IT RUN OFF!
OKAY!
IT'S JUST, I DON'T KNOW...
OTUS...
DON'T YOU THINK IT'S A LITTLE... CONVENIENT THAT THE HIND IS JUST PRESENTING ITSELF LIKE THIS?
SEEMS LIKE MAYBE SOME SORT OF OLYMPIAN TRICK...
WHAT?! WHAT ARE YOU SAYING EPHIALTES? JUST BECAUSE HERA DOESN'T LIKE YOU, DON'T RUIN THINGS FOR ME!
I'M NOT RUINING ANYTHING! IT JUST SEEMS—
HOLD STILL! YOU'LL SCARE HIM!
HUP!

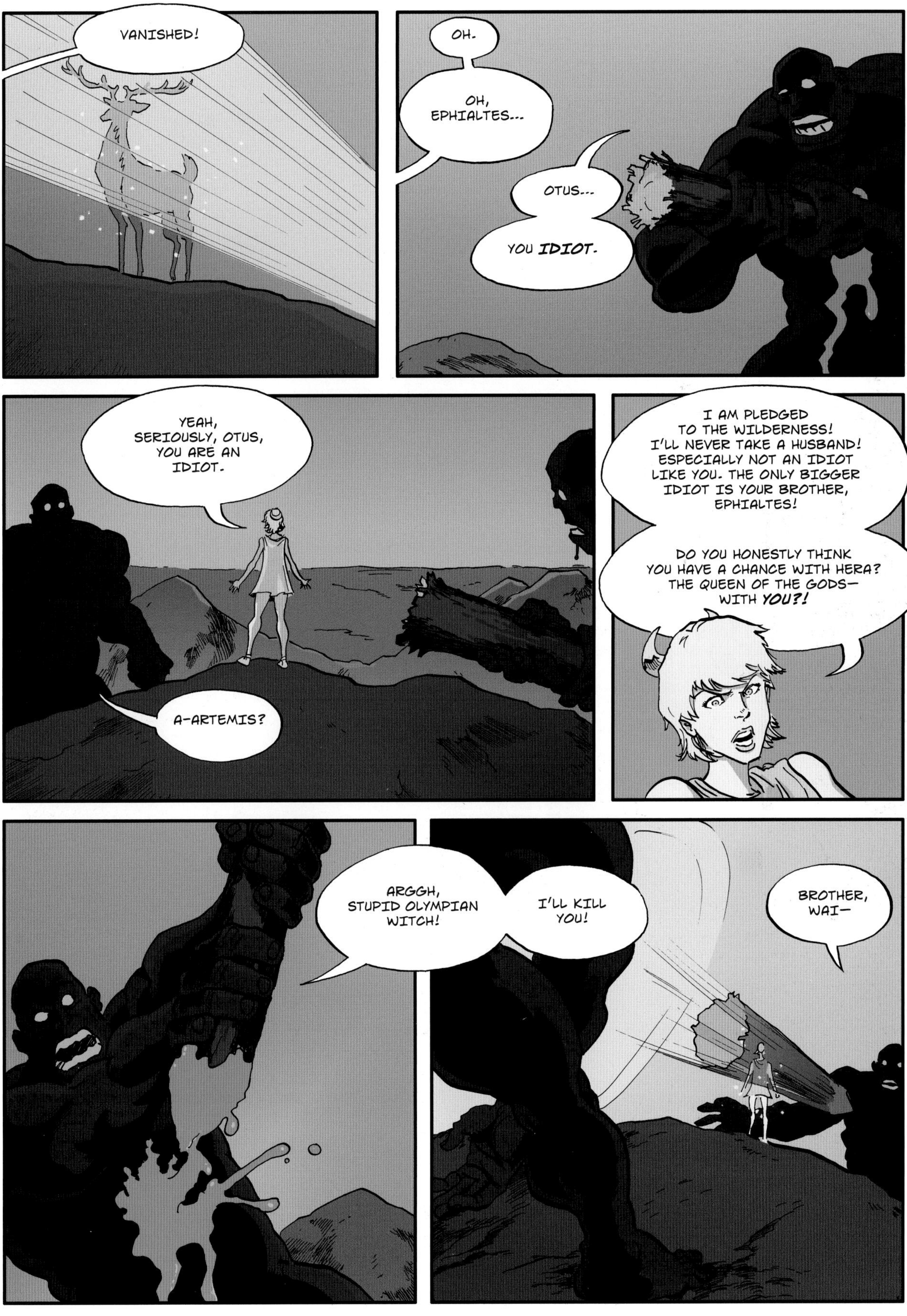
VANISHED!
OH.
OH, EPHIALTES...
OTUS...
YOU **IDIOT**.
YEAH, SERIOUSLY, OTUS, YOU ARE AN IDIOT.
A-ARTEMIS?
I AM PLEDGED TO THE WILDERNESS! I'LL NEVER TAKE A HUSBAND! ESPECIALLY NOT AN IDIOT LIKE YOU. THE ONLY BIGGER IDIOT IS YOUR BROTHER, EPHIALTES!
DO YOU HONESTLY THINK YOU HAVE A CHANCE WITH HERA? THE QUEEN OF THE GODS— WITH ***YOU?!***
ARGGH, STUPID OLYMPIAN WITCH!
I'LL KILL YOU!
BROTHER, WAI—

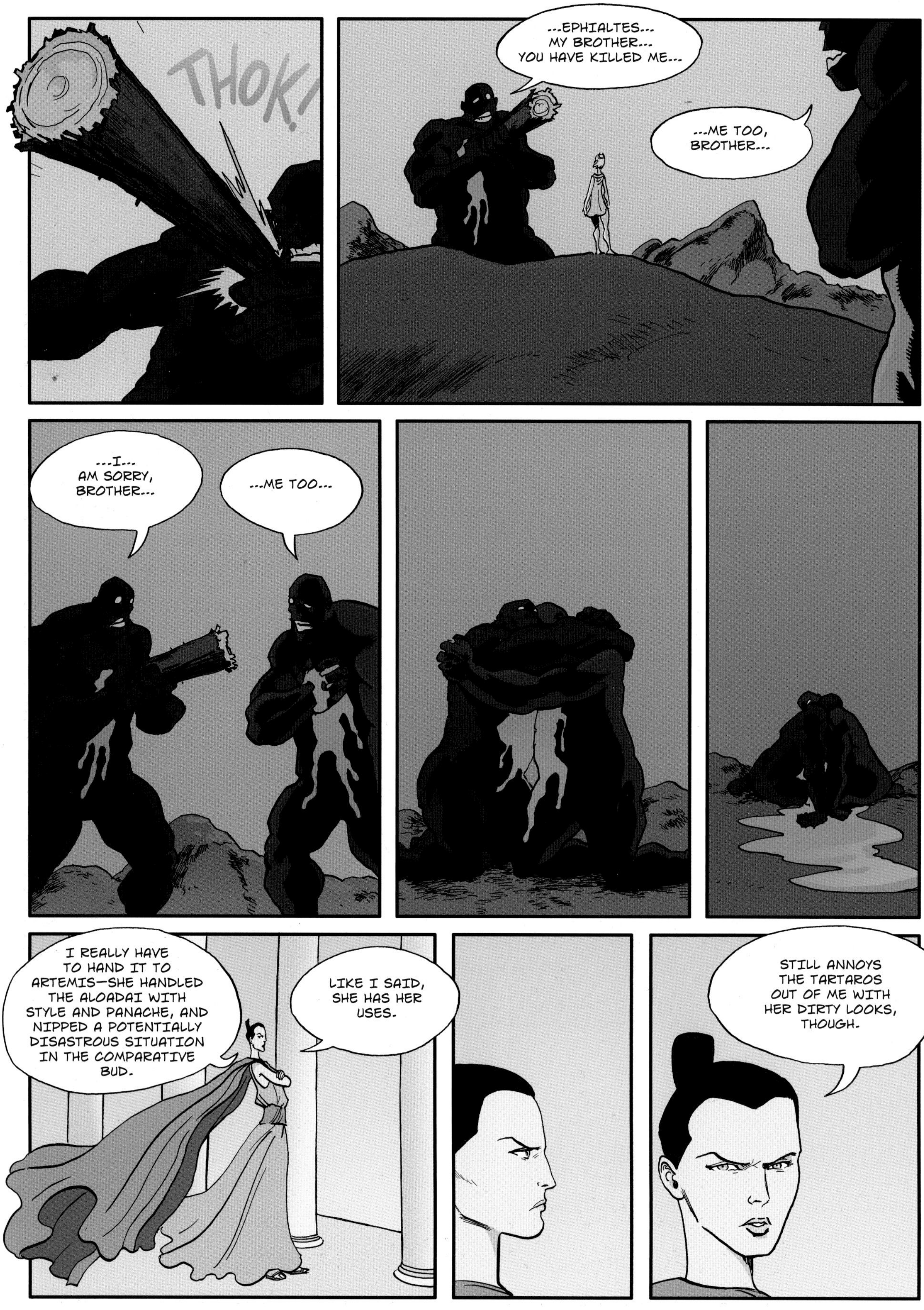
THOK!
...EPHIALTES... MY BROTHER... YOU HAVE KILLED ME...
...ME TOO, BROTHER...
...I... AM SORRY, BROTHER...
...ME TOO...
I REALLY HAVE TO HAND IT TO ARTEMIS—SHE HANDLED THE ALOADAI WITH STYLE AND PANACHE, AND NIPPED A POTENTIALLY DISASTROUS SITUATION IN THE COMPARATIVE BUD.
LIKE I SAID, SHE HAS HER USES.
STILL ANNOYS THE TARTAROS OUT OF ME WITH HER DIRTY LOOKS, THOUGH.

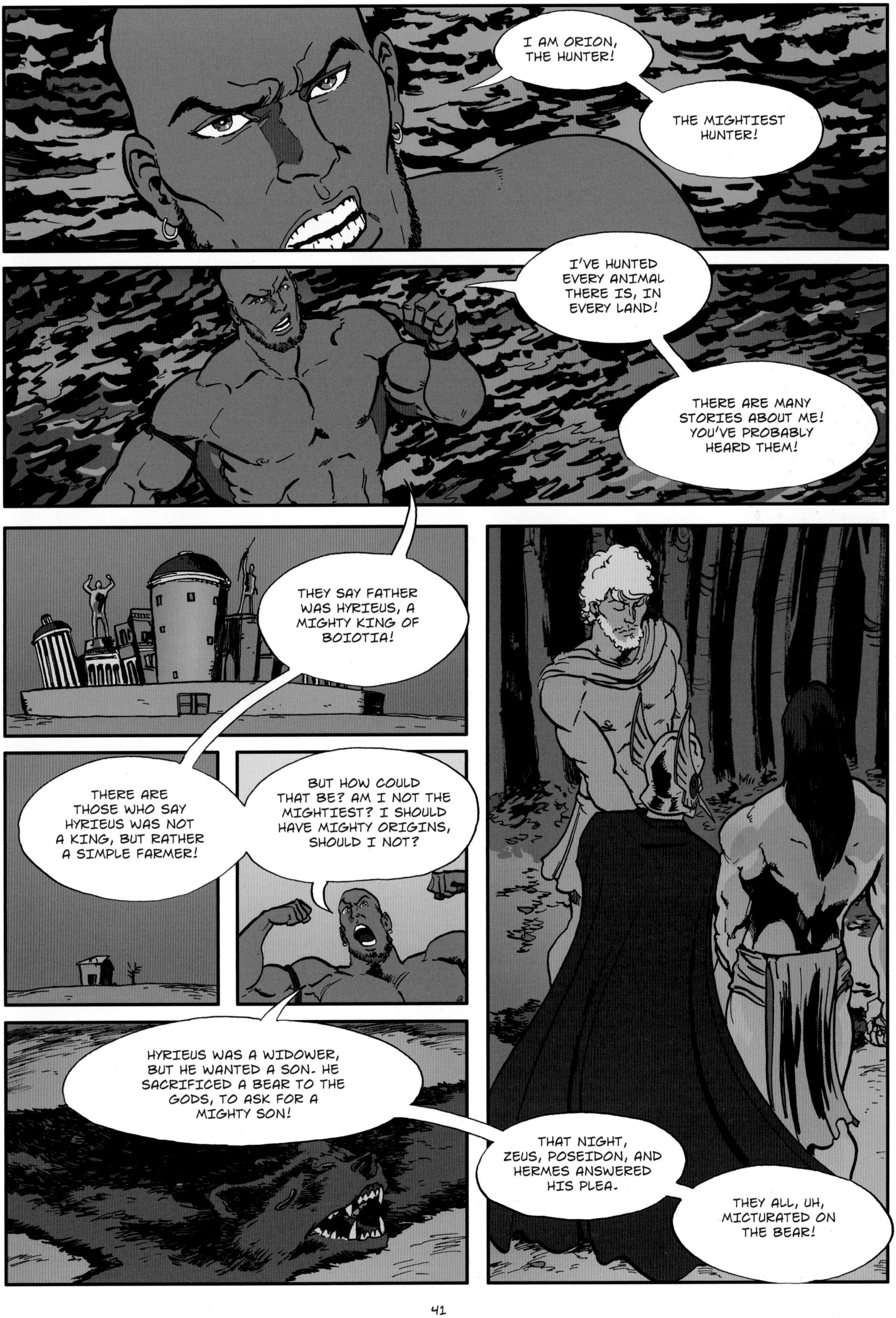
I AM ORION, THE HUNTER!
THE MIGHTIEST HUNTER!
I'VE HUNTED EVERY ANIMAL THERE IS, IN EVERY LAND!
THERE ARE MANY STORIES ABOUT ME! YOU'VE PROBABLY HEARD THEM!
THEY SAY FATHER WAS HYRIEUS, A MIGHTY KING OF BOIOTIA!
THERE ARE THOSE WHO SAY HYRIEUS WAS NOT A KING, BUT RATHER A SIMPLE FARMER!
BUT HOW COULD THAT BE? AM I NOT THE MIGHTIEST? I SHOULD HAVE MIGHTY ORIGINS, SHOULD I NOT?
HYRIEUS WAS A WIDOWER, BUT HE WANTED A SON. HE SACRIFICED A BEAR TO THE GODS, TO ASK FOR A MIGHTY SON!
THAT NIGHT, ZEUS, POSEIDON, AND HERMES ANSWERED HIS PLEA.
THEY ALL, UH, MICTURATED ON THE BEAR!

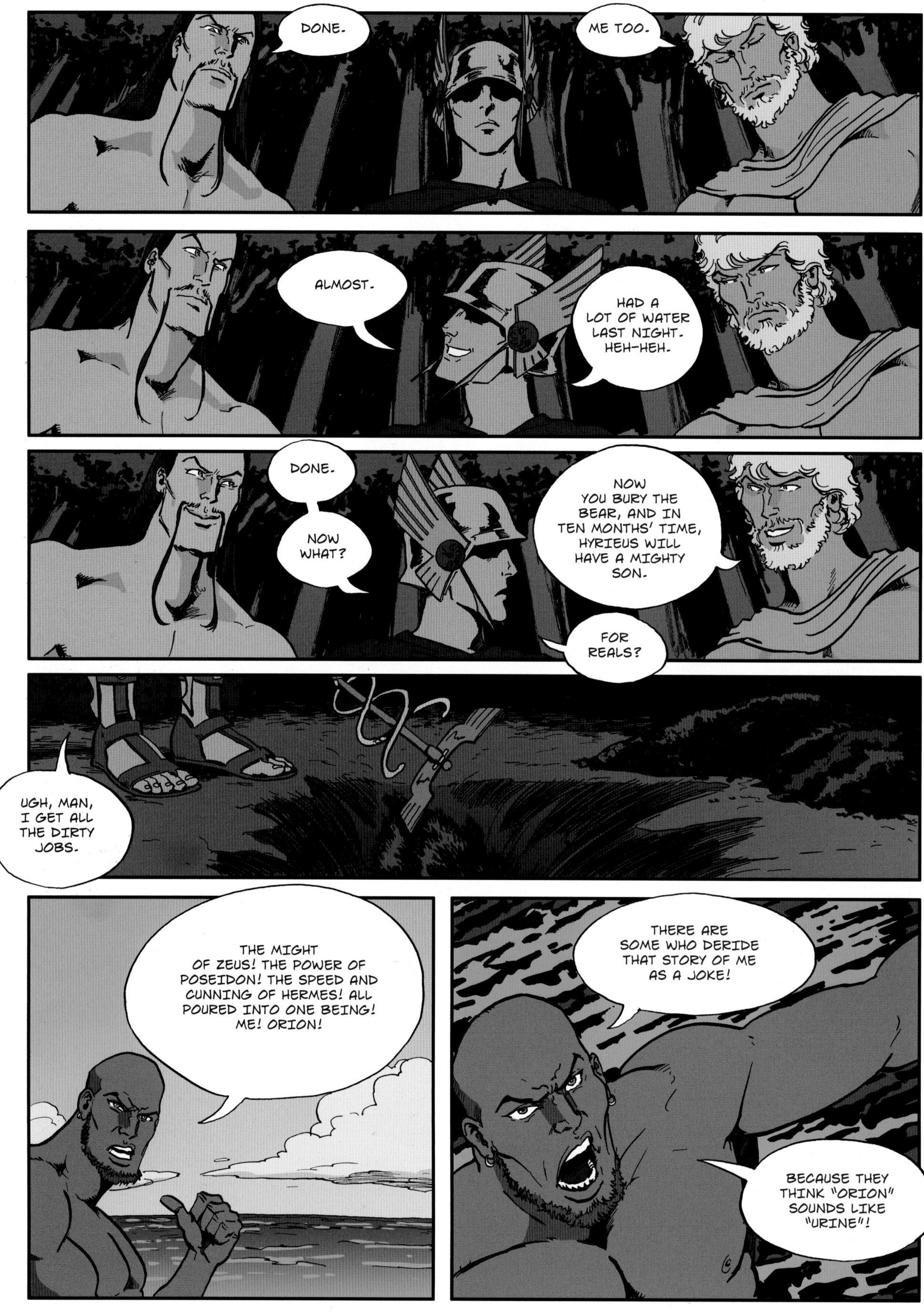
DONE.
ME TOO.
ALMOST.
HAD A LOT OF WATER LAST NIGHT. HEH-HEH.
DONE.
NOW WHAT?
NOW YOU BURY THE BEAR, AND IN TEN MONTHS' TIME, HYRIEUS WILL HAVE A MIGHTY SON.
FOR REALS?
UGH, MAN, I GET ALL THE DIRTY JOBS.
THE MIGHT OF ZEUS! THE POWER OF POSEIDON! THE SPEED AND CUNNING OF HERMES! ALL POURED INTO ONE BEING! ME! ORION!
THERE ARE SOME WHO DERIDE THAT STORY OF ME AS A JOKE!
BECAUSE THEY THINK "ORION" SOUNDS LIKE "URINE"!

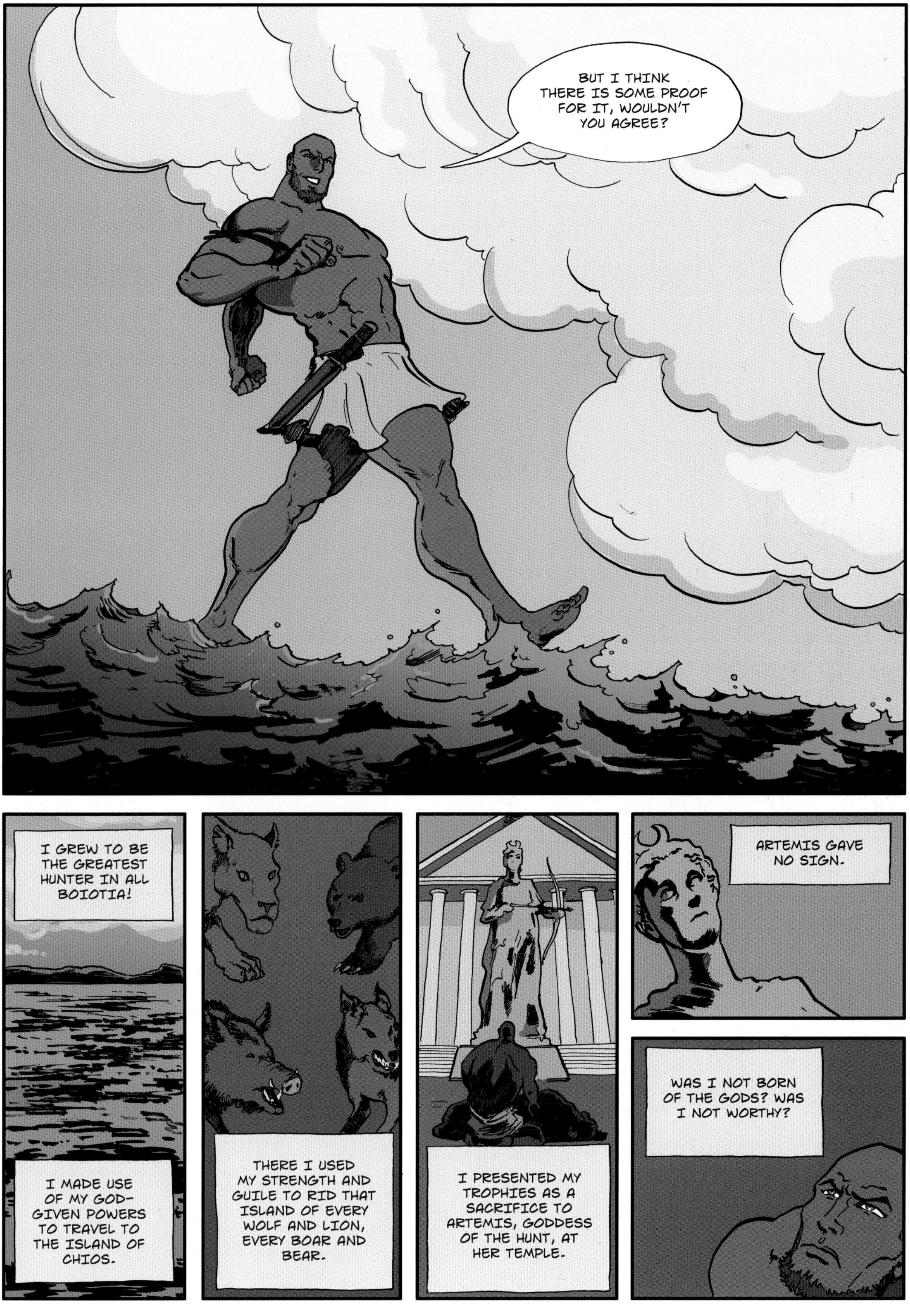
BUT I THINK THERE IS SOME PROOF FOR IT, WOULDN'T YOU AGREE?
I GREW TO BE THE GREATEST HUNTER IN ALL BOIOTIA!
I MADE USE OF MY GOD-GIVEN POWERS TO TRAVEL TO THE ISLAND OF CHIOS.
THERE I USED MY STRENGTH AND GUILE TO RID THAT ISLAND OF EVERY WOLF AND LION, EVERY BOAR AND BEAR.
I PRESENTED MY TROPHIES AS A SACRIFICE TO ARTEMIS, GODDESS OF THE HUNT, AT HER TEMPLE.
ARTEMIS GAVE NO SIGN.
WAS I NOT BORN OF THE GODS? WAS I NOT WORTHY?

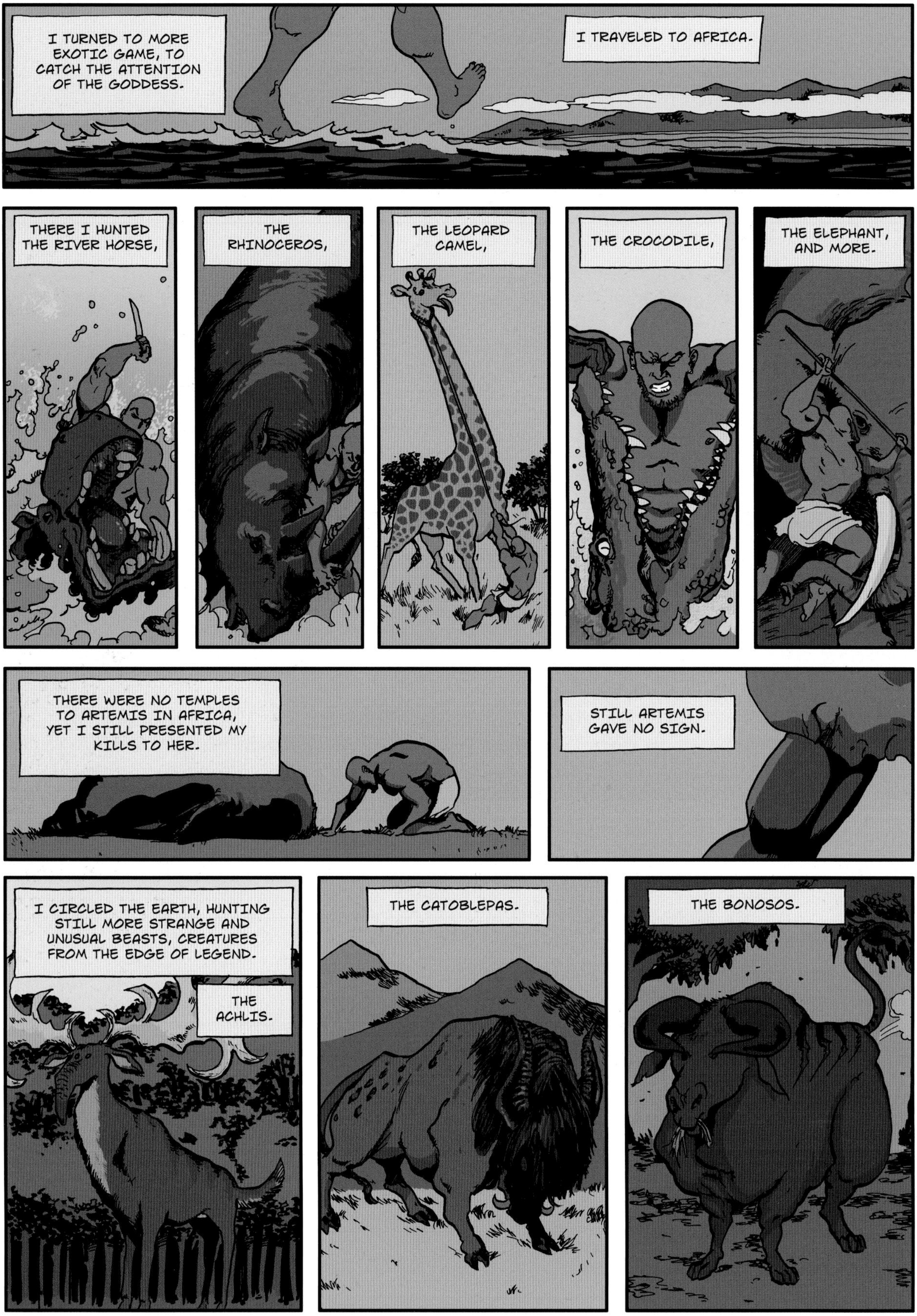
I TURNED TO MORE EXOTIC GAME, TO CATCH THE ATTENTION OF THE GODDESS.
I TRAVELED TO AFRICA.
THERE I HUNTED THE RIVER HORSE,
THE RHINOCEROS,
THE LEOPARD CAMEL,
THE CROCODILE,
THE ELEPHANT, AND MORE.
THERE WERE NO TEMPLES TO ARTEMIS IN AFRICA, YET I STILL PRESENTED MY KILLS TO HER.
STILL ARTEMIS GAVE NO SIGN.
I CIRCLED THE EARTH, HUNTING STILL MORE STRANGE AND UNUSUAL BEASTS, CREATURES FROM THE EDGE OF LEGEND.
THE ACHLIS.
THE CATOBLEPAS.
THE BONOSOS.

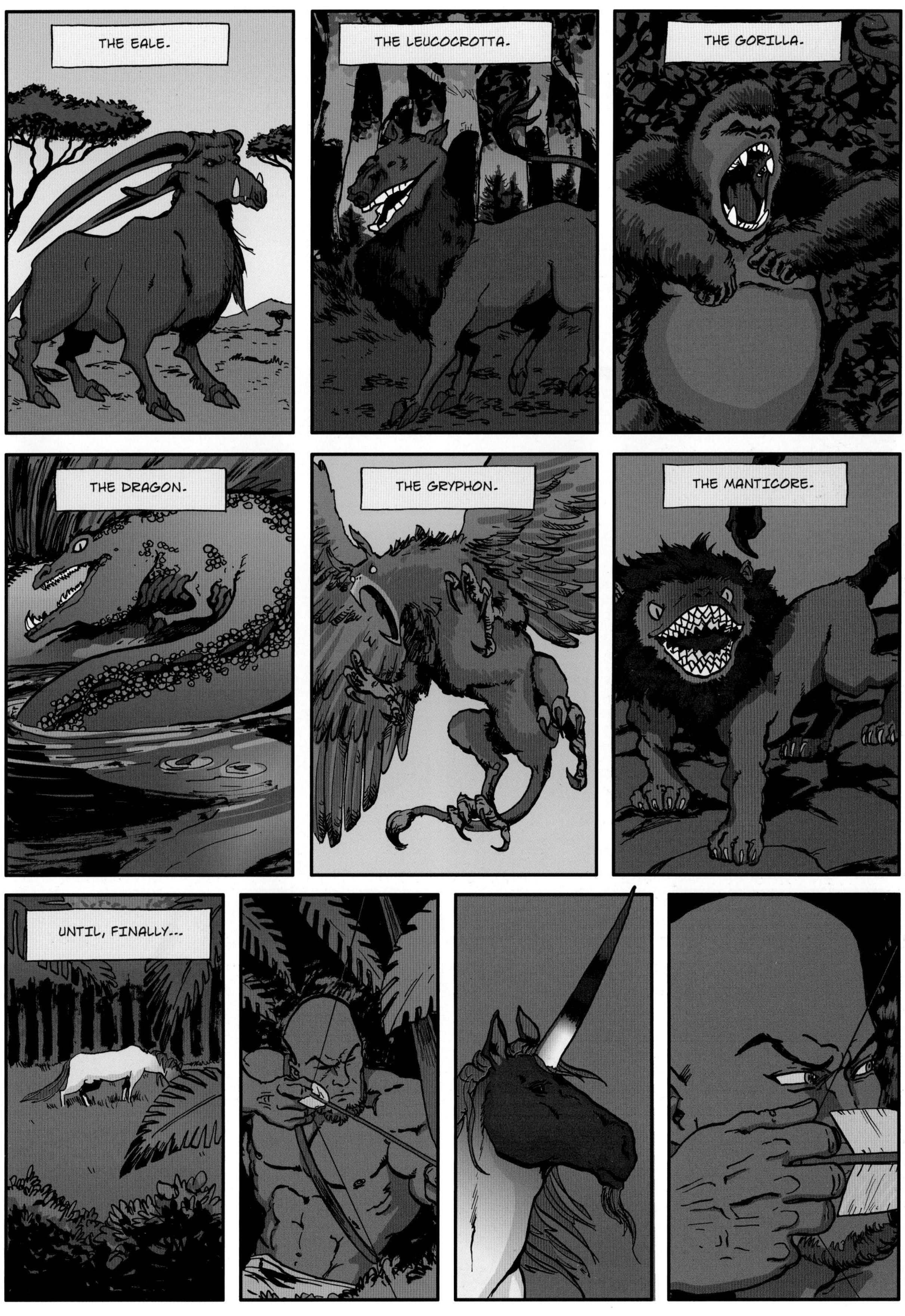
THE EALE.
THE LEUCOCROTTA.
THE GORILLA.
THE DRAGON.
THE GRYPHON.
THE MANTICORE.
UNTIL, FINALLY...

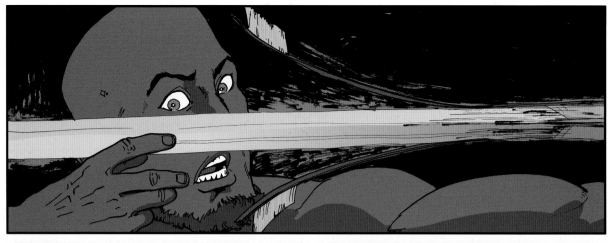

CATCH ME
IF YOU CAN.

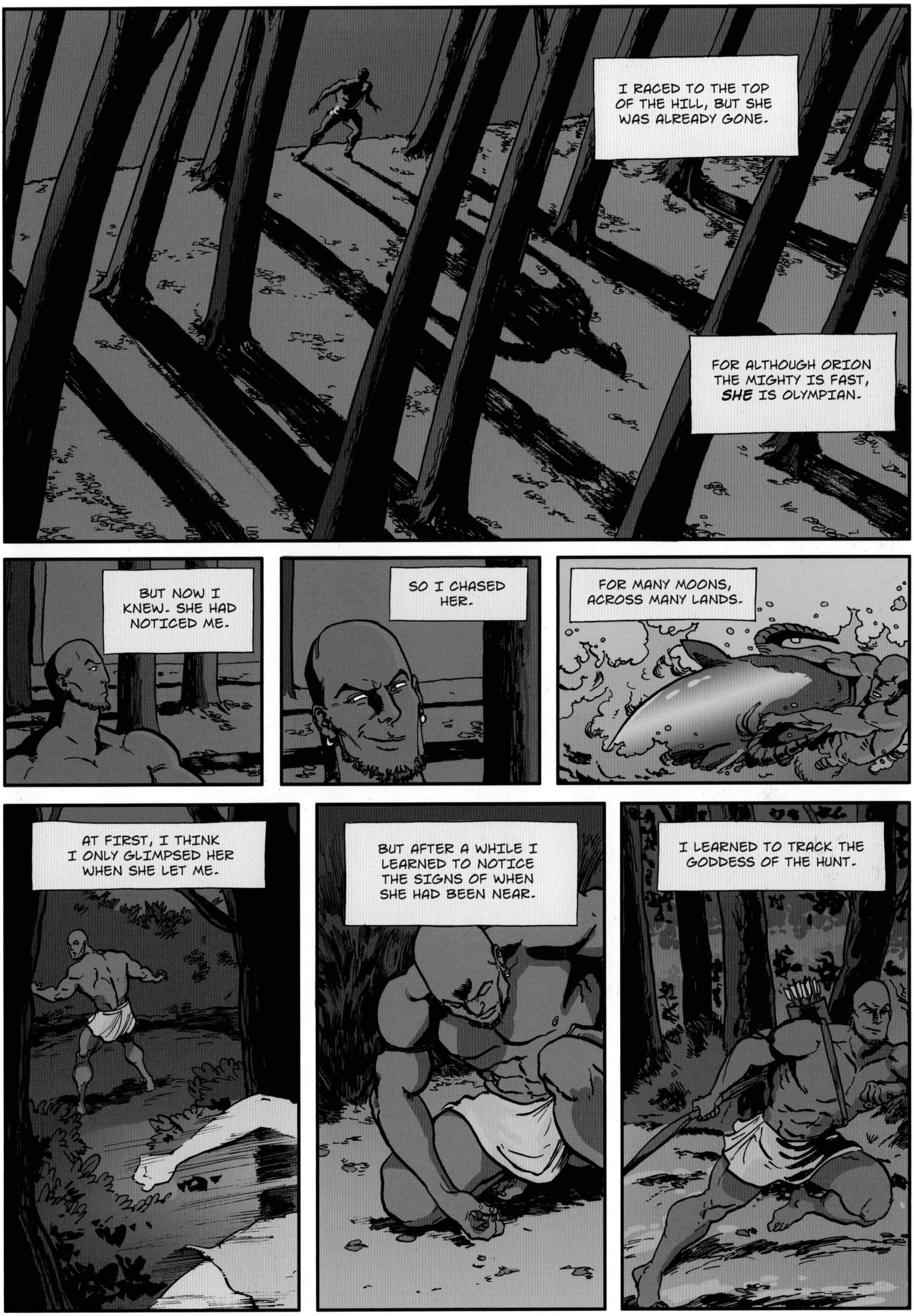
I RACED TO THE TOP OF THE HILL, BUT SHE WAS ALREADY GONE.
FOR ALTHOUGH ORION THE MIGHTY IS FAST, **SHE** IS OLYMPIAN.
BUT NOW I KNEW. SHE HAD NOTICED ME.
SO I CHASED HER.
FOR MANY MOONS, ACROSS MANY LANDS.
AT FIRST, I THINK I ONLY GLIMPSED HER WHEN SHE LET ME.
BUT AFTER A WHILE I LEARNED TO NOTICE THE SIGNS OF WHEN SHE HAD BEEN NEAR.
I LEARNED TO TRACK THE GODDESS OF THE HUNT.

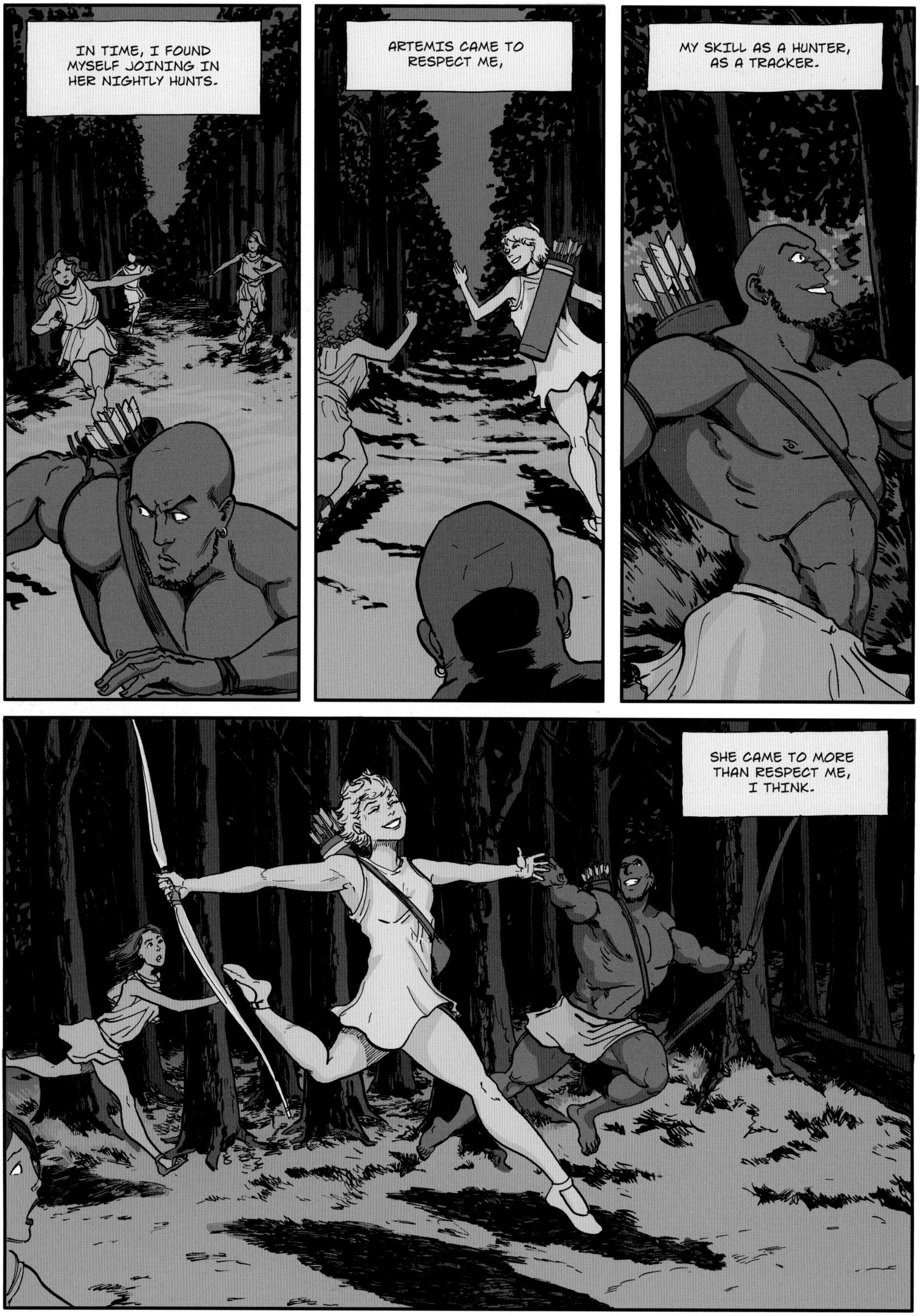
IN TIME, I FOUND MYSELF JOINING IN HER NIGHTLY HUNTS.
ARTEMIS CAME TO RESPECT ME,
MY SKILL AS A HUNTER, AS A TRACKER.
SHE CAME TO MORE THAN RESPECT ME, I THINK.

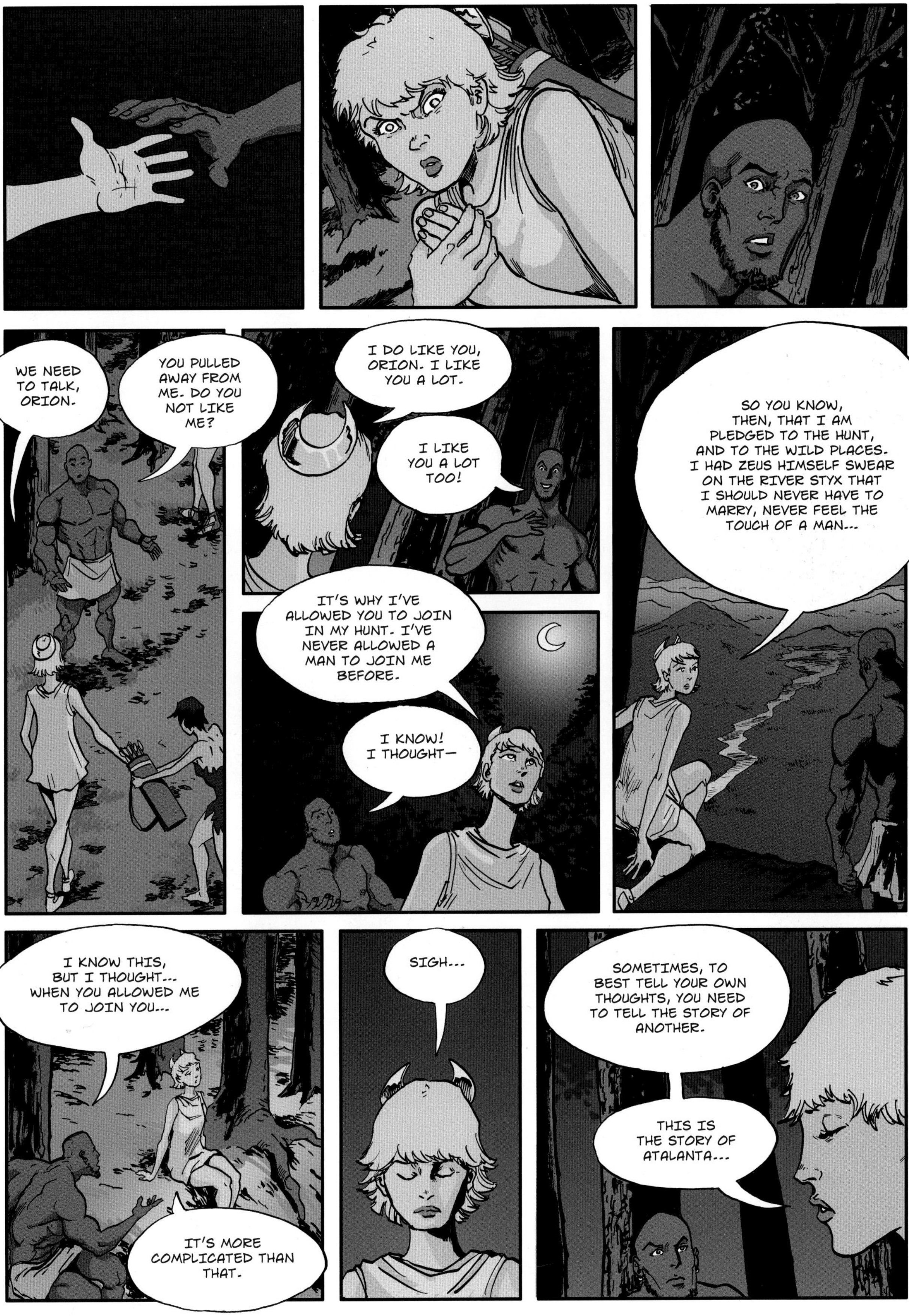
WE NEED TO TALK, ORION.
YOU PULLED AWAY FROM ME. DO YOU NOT LIKE ME?
I DO LIKE YOU, ORION. I LIKE YOU A LOT.
I LIKE YOU A LOT TOO!
IT'S WHY I'VE ALLOWED YOU TO JOIN IN MY HUNT. I'VE NEVER ALLOWED A MAN TO JOIN ME BEFORE.
I KNOW! I THOUGHT—
SO YOU KNOW, THEN, THAT I AM PLEDGED TO THE HUNT, AND TO THE WILD PLACES. I HAD ZEUS HIMSELF SWEAR ON THE RIVER STYX THAT I SHOULD NEVER HAVE TO MARRY, NEVER FEEL THE TOUCH OF A MAN...
I KNOW THIS, BUT I THOUGHT... WHEN YOU ALLOWED ME TO JOIN YOU...
IT'S MORE COMPLICATED THAN THAT.
SIGH...
SOMETIMES, TO BEST TELL YOUR OWN THOUGHTS, YOU NEED TO TELL THE STORY OF ANOTHER.
THIS IS THE STORY OF ATALANTA...

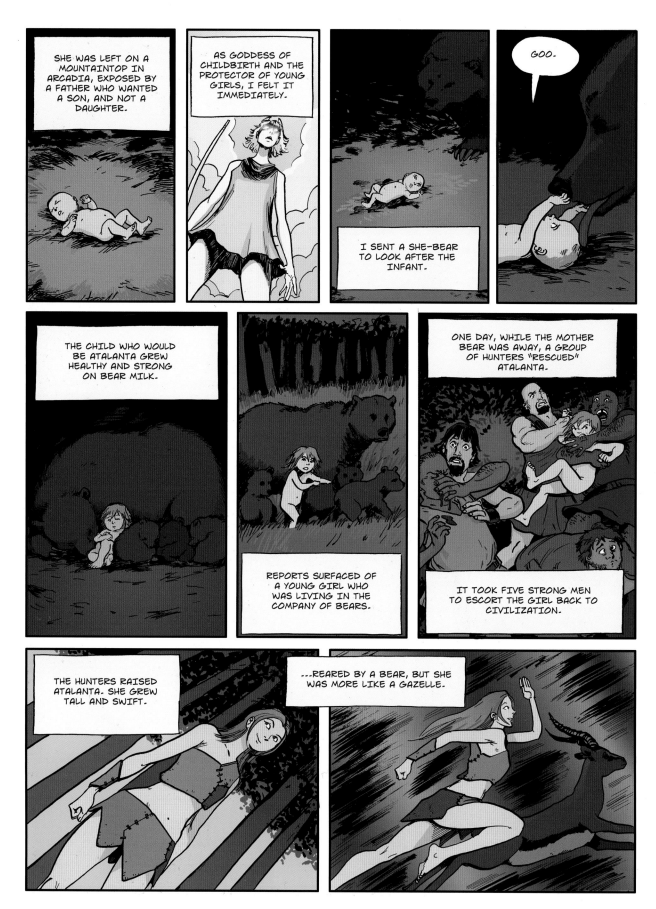

SHE WAS LEFT ON A MOUNTAINTOP IN ARCADIA, EXPOSED BY A FATHER WHO WANTED A SON, AND NOT A DAUGHTER.

AS GODDESS OF CHILDBIRTH AND THE PROTECTOR OF YOUNG GIRLS, I FELT IT IMMEDIATELY.

GOO.

I SENT A SHE-BEAR TO LOOK AFTER THE INFANT.

THE CHILD WHO WOULD BE ATALANTA GREW HEALTHY AND STRONG ON BEAR MILK.

REPORTS SURFACED OF A YOUNG GIRL WHO WAS LIVING IN THE COMPANY OF BEARS.

ONE DAY, WHILE THE MOTHER BEAR WAS AWAY, A GROUP OF HUNTERS "RESCUED" ATALANTA.

IT TOOK FIVE STRONG MEN TO ESCORT THE GIRL BACK TO CIVILIZATION.

THE HUNTERS RAISED ATALANTA. SHE GREW TALL AND SWIFT.

...REARED BY A BEAR, BUT SHE WAS MORE LIKE A GAZELLE.

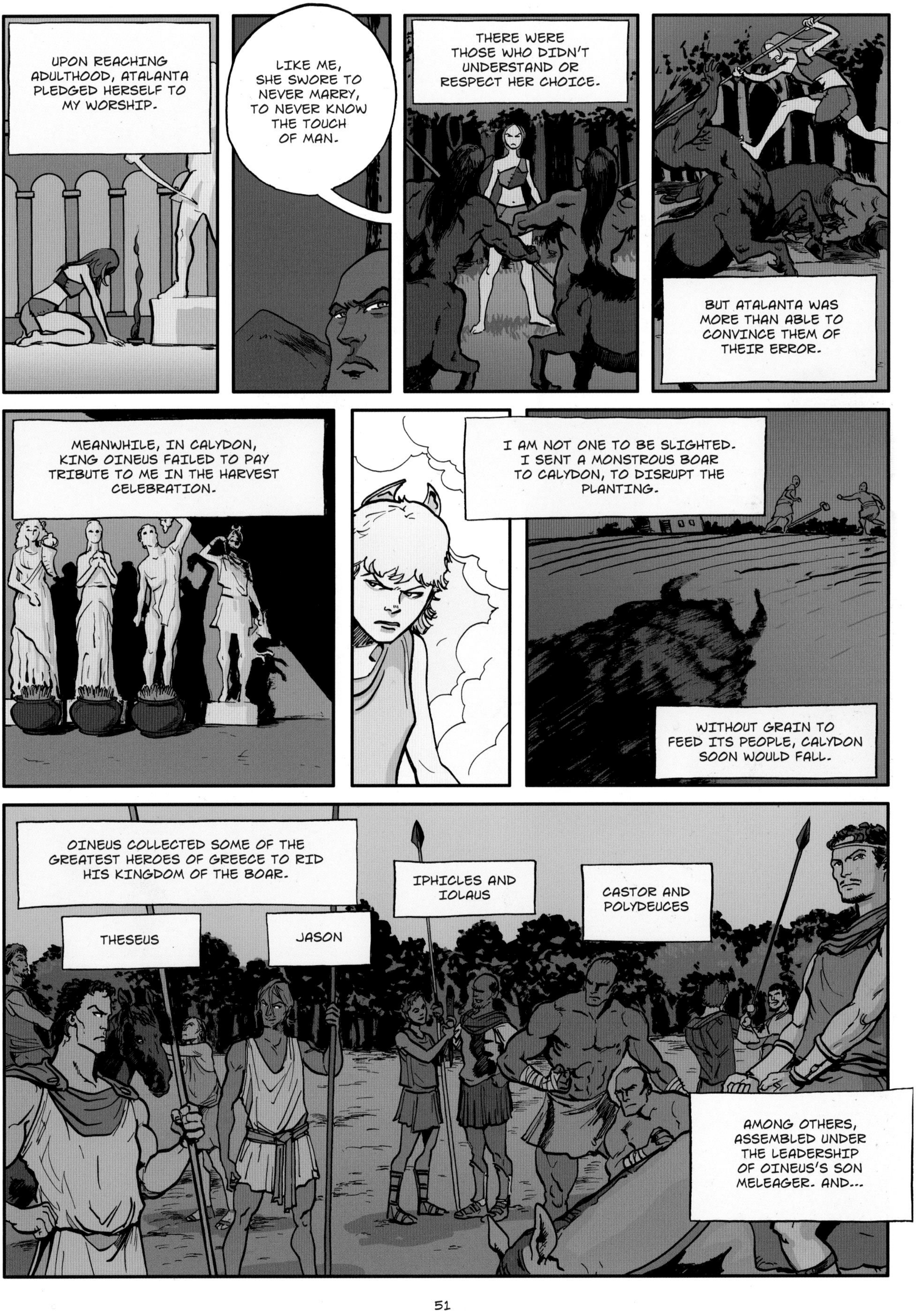
UPON REACHING ADULTHOOD, ATALANTA PLEDGED HERSELF TO MY WORSHIP.
LIKE ME, SHE SWORE TO NEVER MARRY, TO NEVER KNOW THE TOUCH OF MAN.
THERE WERE THOSE WHO DIDN'T UNDERSTAND OR RESPECT HER CHOICE.
BUT ATALANTA WAS MORE THAN ABLE TO CONVINCE THEM OF THEIR ERROR.
MEANWHILE, IN CALYDON, KING OINEUS FAILED TO PAY TRIBUTE TO ME IN THE HARVEST CELEBRATION.
I AM NOT ONE TO BE SLIGHTED. I SENT A MONSTROUS BOAR TO CALYDON, TO DISRUPT THE PLANTING.
WITHOUT GRAIN TO FEED ITS PEOPLE, CALYDON SOON WOULD FALL.
OINEUS COLLECTED SOME OF THE GREATEST HEROES OF GREECE TO RID HIS KINGDOM OF THE BOAR.
THESEUS
JASON
IPHICLES AND IOLAUS
CASTOR AND POLYDEUCES
AMONG OTHERS, ASSEMBLED UNDER THE LEADERSHIP OF OINEUS'S SON MELEAGER. AND...

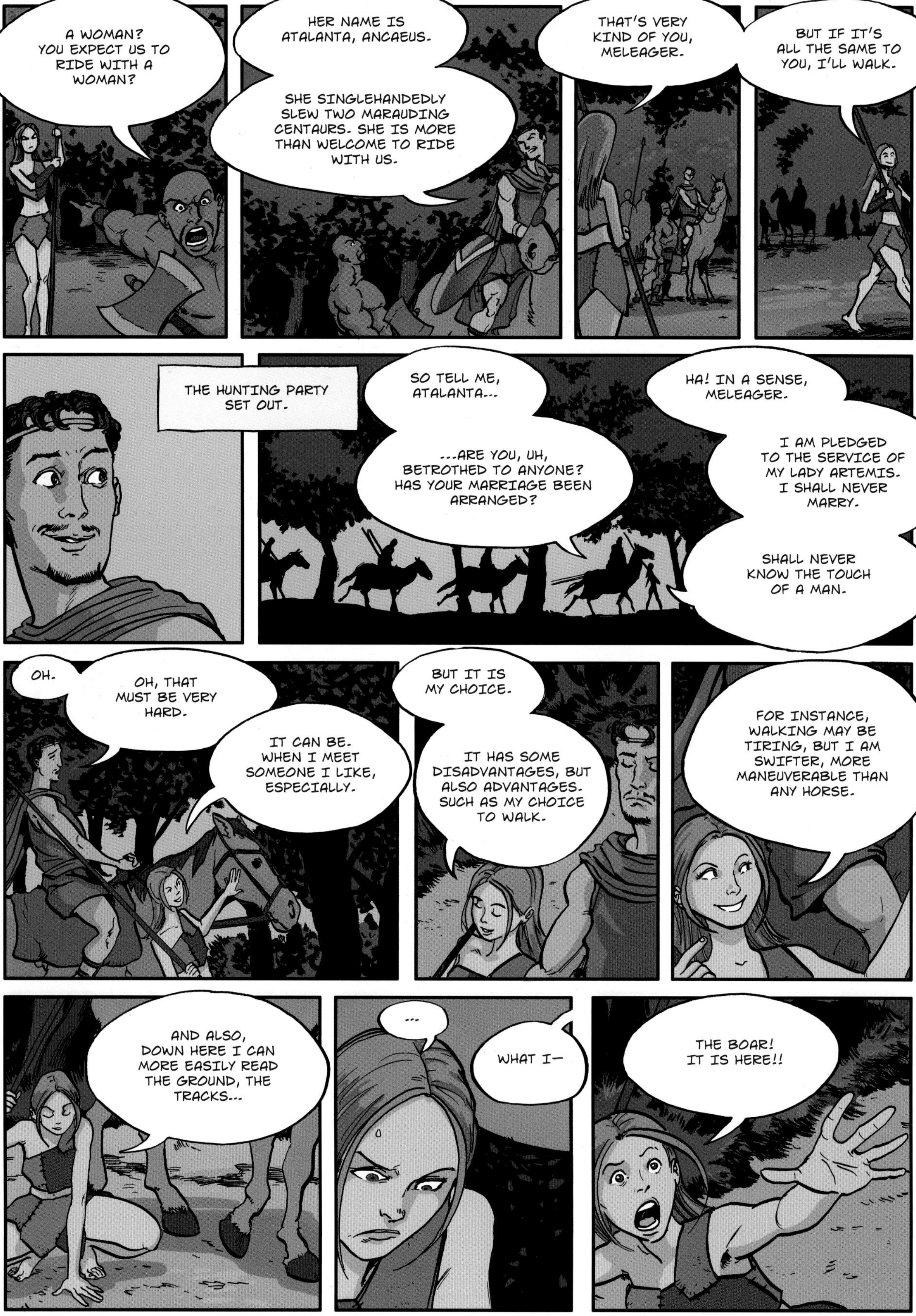
A WOMAN? YOU EXPECT US TO RIDE WITH A WOMAN?
HER NAME IS ATALANTA, ANCAEUS.
SHE SINGLEHANDEDLY SLEW TWO MARAUDING CENTAURS. SHE IS MORE THAN WELCOME TO RIDE WITH US.
THAT'S VERY KIND OF YOU, MELEAGER.
BUT IF IT'S ALL THE SAME TO YOU, I'LL WALK.
THE HUNTING PARTY SET OUT.
SO TELL ME, ATALANTA...
...ARE YOU, UH, BETROTHED TO ANYONE? HAS YOUR MARRIAGE BEEN ARRANGED?
HA! IN A SENSE, MELEAGER.
I AM PLEDGED TO THE SERVICE OF MY LADY ARTEMIS. I SHALL NEVER MARRY.
SHALL NEVER KNOW THE TOUCH OF A MAN.
OH.
OH, THAT MUST BE VERY HARD.
IT CAN BE. WHEN I MEET SOMEONE I LIKE, ESPECIALLY.
BUT IT IS MY CHOICE.
IT HAS SOME DISADVANTAGES, BUT ALSO ADVANTAGES. SUCH AS MY CHOICE TO WALK.
FOR INSTANCE, WALKING MAY BE TIRING, BUT I AM SWIFTER, MORE MANEUVERABLE THAN ANY HORSE.
AND ALSO, DOWN HERE I CAN MORE EASILY READ THE GROUND, THE TRACKS...
...
WHAT I—
THE BOAR! IT IS HERE!!

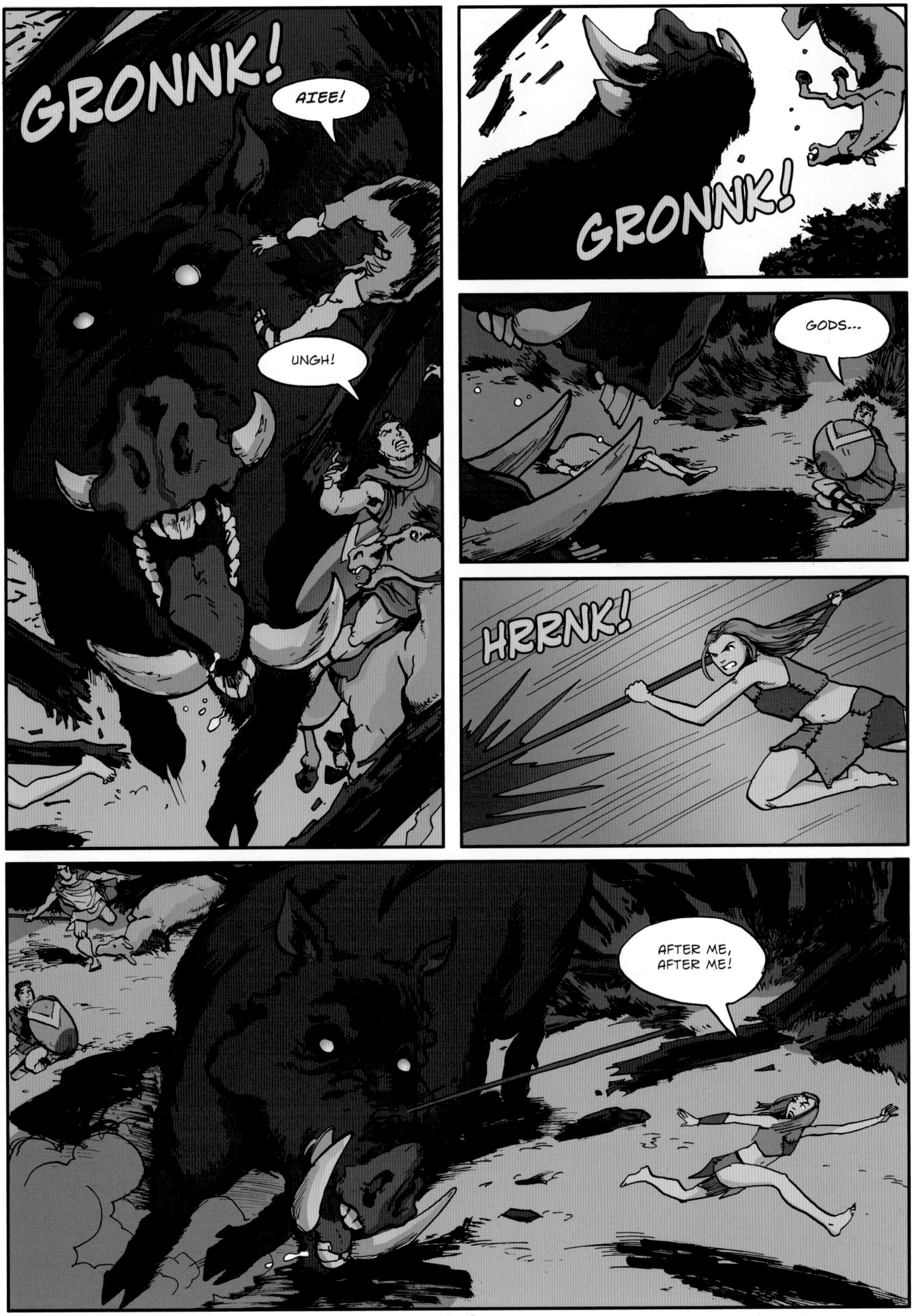
GRONNK!
AIEE!
UNGH!
GRONNK!
GODS...
HRRNK!
AFTER ME, AFTER ME!

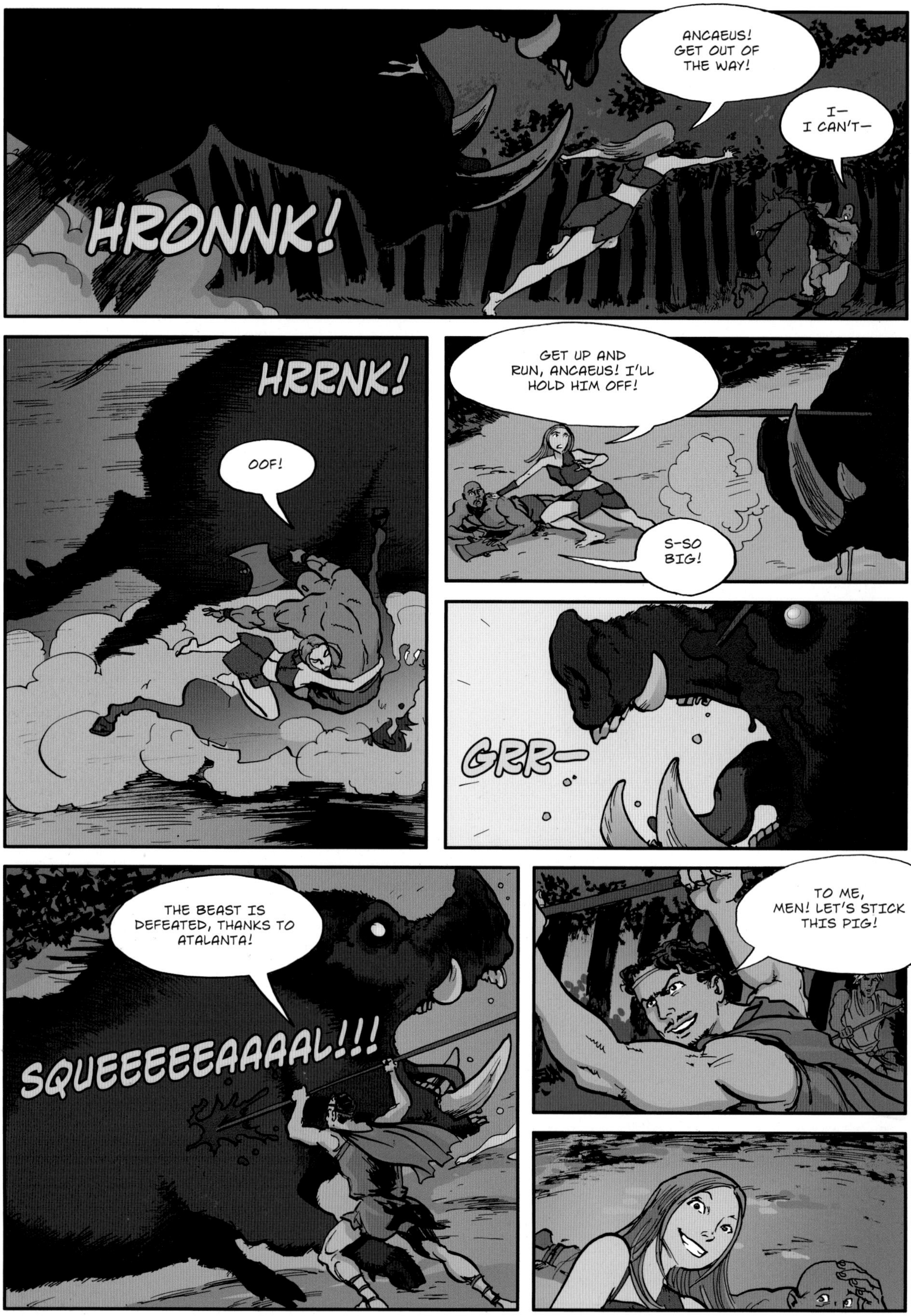
ANCAEUS! GET OUT OF THE WAY!
I— I CAN'T—
HRONNK!
HRRNK!
OOF!
GET UP AND RUN, ANCAEUS! I'LL HOLD HIM OFF!
S-SO BIG!
GRR—
THE BEAST IS DEFEATED, THANKS TO ATALANTA!
SQUEEEEEEAAAAL!!!
TO ME, MEN! LET'S STICK THIS PIG!

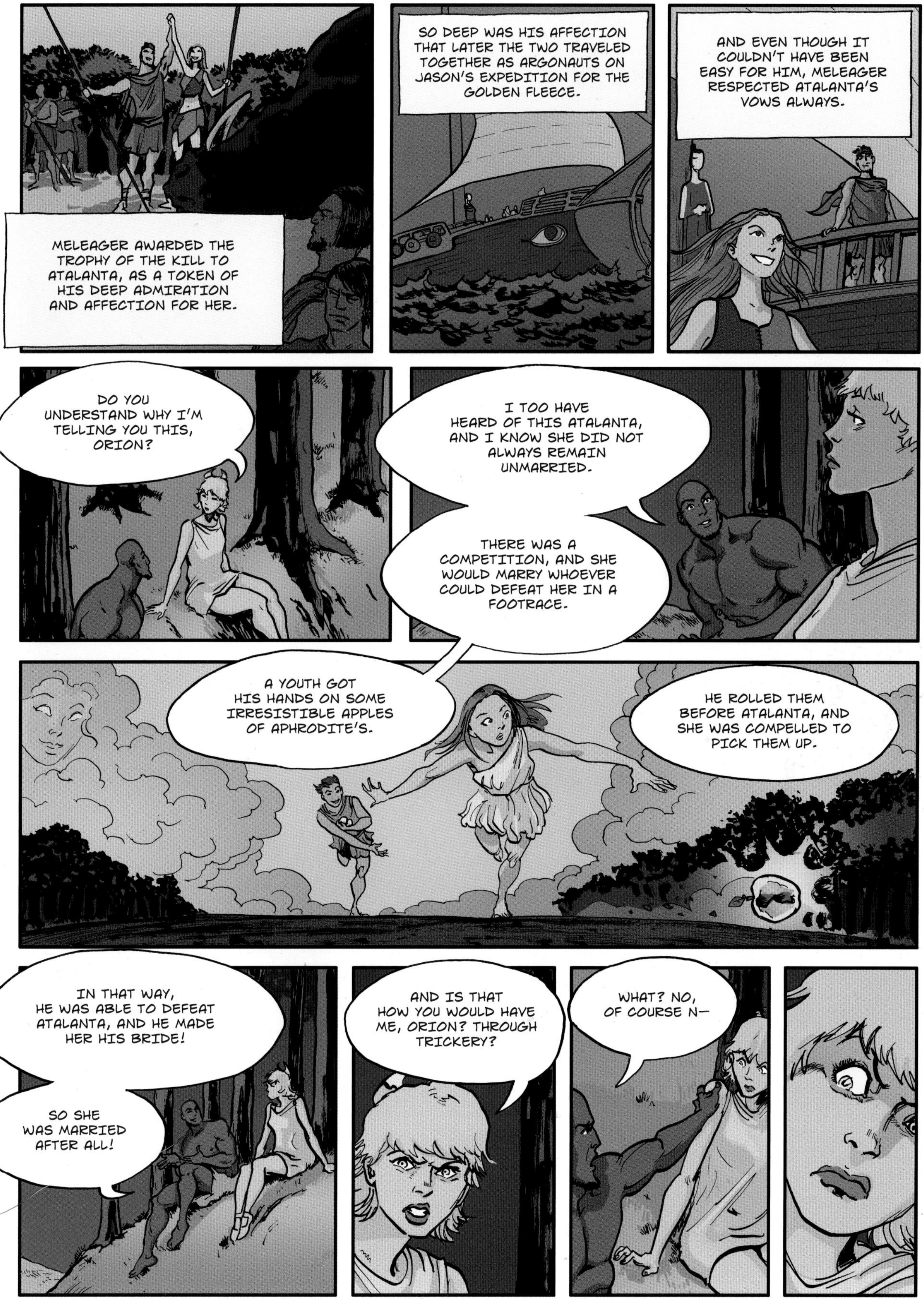
MELEAGER AWARDED THE TROPHY OF THE KILL TO ATALANTA, AS A TOKEN OF HIS DEEP ADMIRATION AND AFFECTION FOR HER.
SO DEEP WAS HIS AFFECTION THAT LATER THE TWO TRAVELED TOGETHER AS ARGONAUTS ON JASON'S EXPEDITION FOR THE GOLDEN FLEECE.
AND EVEN THOUGH IT COULDN'T HAVE BEEN EASY FOR HIM, MELEAGER RESPECTED ATALANTA'S VOWS ALWAYS.
DO YOU UNDERSTAND WHY I'M TELLING YOU THIS, ORION?
I TOO HAVE HEARD OF THIS ATALANTA, AND I KNOW SHE DID NOT ALWAYS REMAIN UNMARRIED.
THERE WAS A COMPETITION, AND SHE WOULD MARRY WHOEVER COULD DEFEAT HER IN A FOOTRACE.
A YOUTH GOT HIS HANDS ON SOME IRRESISTIBLE APPLES OF APHRODITE'S.
HE ROLLED THEM BEFORE ATALANTA, AND SHE WAS COMPELLED TO PICK THEM UP.
IN THAT WAY, HE WAS ABLE TO DEFEAT ATALANTA, AND HE MADE HER HIS BRIDE!
SO SHE WAS MARRIED AFTER ALL!
AND IS THAT HOW YOU WOULD HAVE ME, ORION? THROUGH TRICKERY?
WHAT? NO, OF COURSE N—

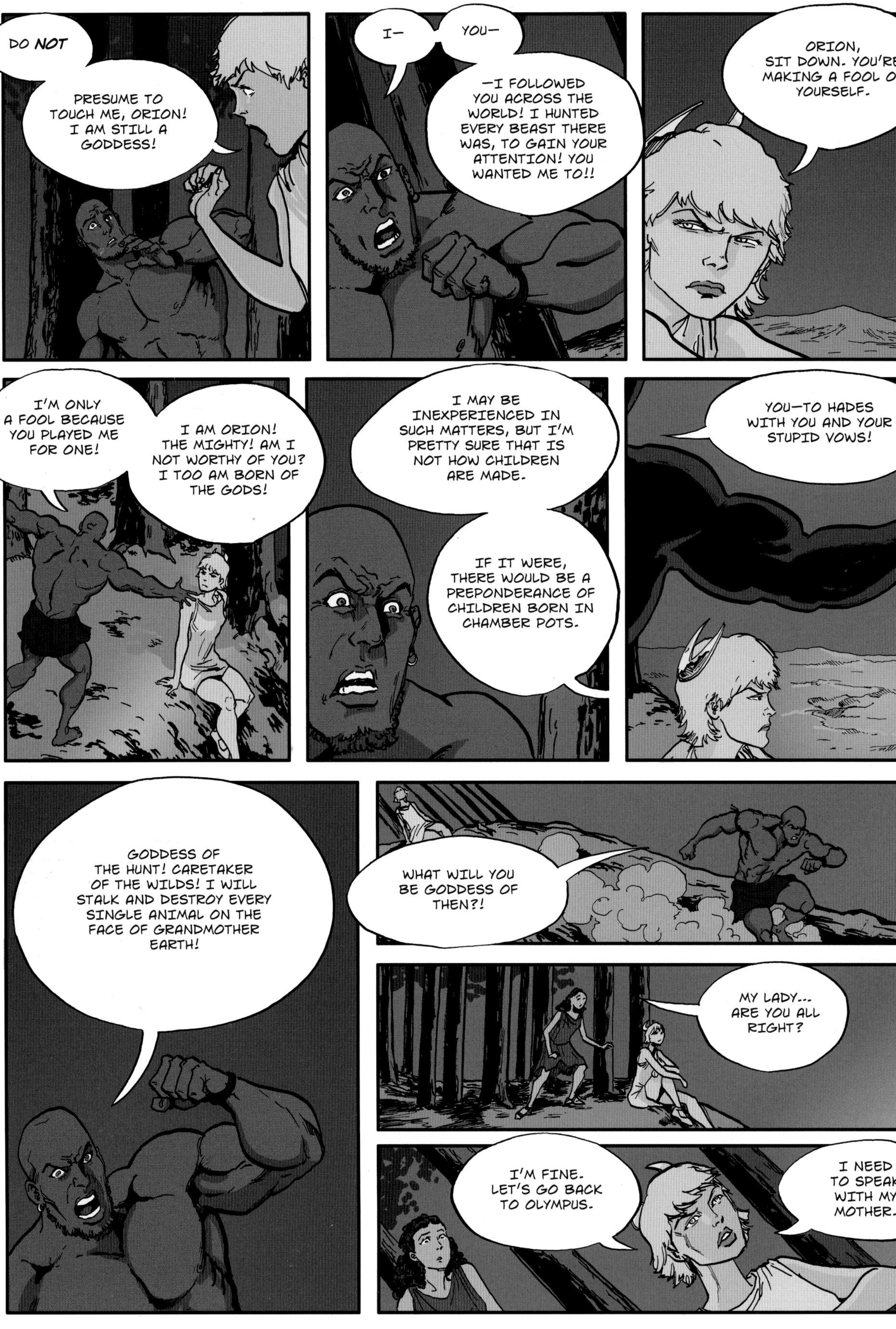
DO NOT
PRESUME TO TOUCH ME, ORION! I AM STILL A GODDESS!
I—
YOU—
—I FOLLOWED YOU ACROSS THE WORLD! I HUNTED EVERY BEAST THERE WAS, TO GAIN YOUR ATTENTION! YOU WANTED ME TO!!
ORION, SIT DOWN. YOU'RE MAKING A FOOL OF YOURSELF.
I'M ONLY A FOOL BECAUSE YOU PLAYED ME FOR ONE!
I AM ORION! THE MIGHTY! AM I NOT WORTHY OF YOU? I TOO AM BORN OF THE GODS!
I MAY BE INEXPERIENCED IN SUCH MATTERS, BUT I'M PRETTY SURE THAT IS NOT HOW CHILDREN ARE MADE.
IF IT WERE, THERE WOULD BE A PREPONDERANCE OF CHILDREN BORN IN CHAMBER POTS.
YOU—TO HADES WITH YOU AND YOUR STUPID VOWS!
GODDESS OF THE HUNT! CARETAKER OF THE WILDS! I WILL STALK AND DESTROY EVERY SINGLE ANIMAL ON THE FACE OF GRANDMOTHER EARTH!
WHAT WILL YOU BE GODDESS OF THEN?!
MY LADY... ARE YOU ALL RIGHT?
I'M FINE. LET'S GO BACK TO OLYMPUS.
I NEED TO SPEAK WITH MY MOTHER.

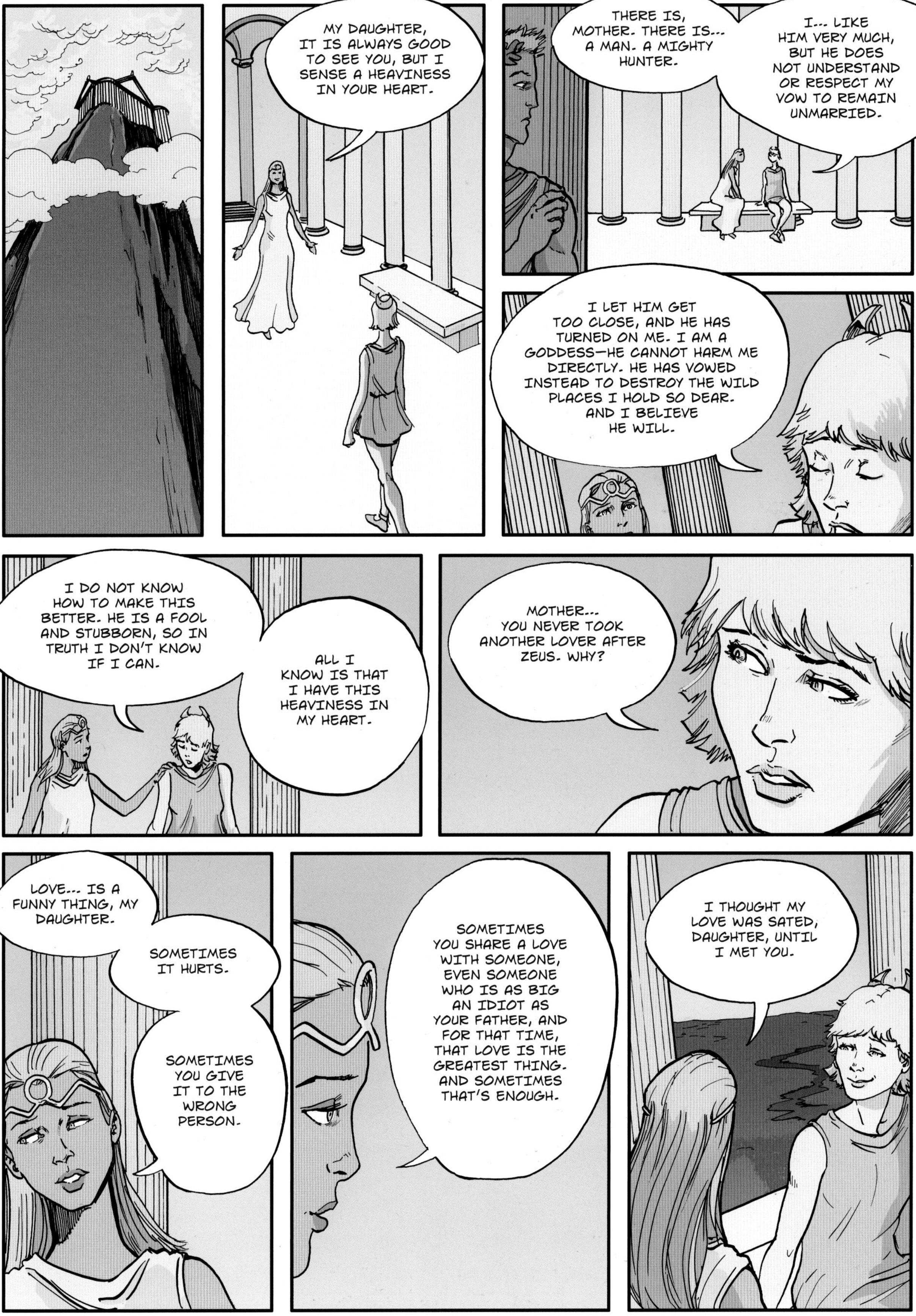
MY DAUGHTER, IT IS ALWAYS GOOD TO SEE YOU, BUT I SENSE A HEAVINESS IN YOUR HEART.
THERE IS, MOTHER. THERE IS... A MAN. A MIGHTY HUNTER.
I... LIKE HIM VERY MUCH, BUT HE DOES NOT UNDERSTAND OR RESPECT MY VOW TO REMAIN UNMARRIED.
I LET HIM GET TOO CLOSE, AND HE HAS TURNED ON ME. I AM A GODDESS—HE CANNOT HARM ME DIRECTLY. HE HAS VOWED INSTEAD TO DESTROY THE WILD PLACES I HOLD SO DEAR. AND I BELIEVE HE WILL.
I DO NOT KNOW HOW TO MAKE THIS BETTER. HE IS A FOOL AND STUBBORN, SO IN TRUTH I DON'T KNOW IF I CAN.
ALL I KNOW IS THAT I HAVE THIS HEAVINESS IN MY HEART.
MOTHER... YOU NEVER TOOK ANOTHER LOVER AFTER ZEUS. WHY?
LOVE... IS A FUNNY THING, MY DAUGHTER.
SOMETIMES IT HURTS.
SOMETIMES YOU GIVE IT TO THE WRONG PERSON.
SOMETIMES YOU SHARE A LOVE WITH SOMEONE, EVEN SOMEONE WHO IS AS BIG AN IDIOT AS YOUR FATHER, AND FOR THAT TIME, THAT LOVE IS THE GREATEST THING. AND SOMETIMES THAT'S ENOUGH.
I THOUGHT MY LOVE WAS SATED, DAUGHTER, UNTIL I MET YOU.

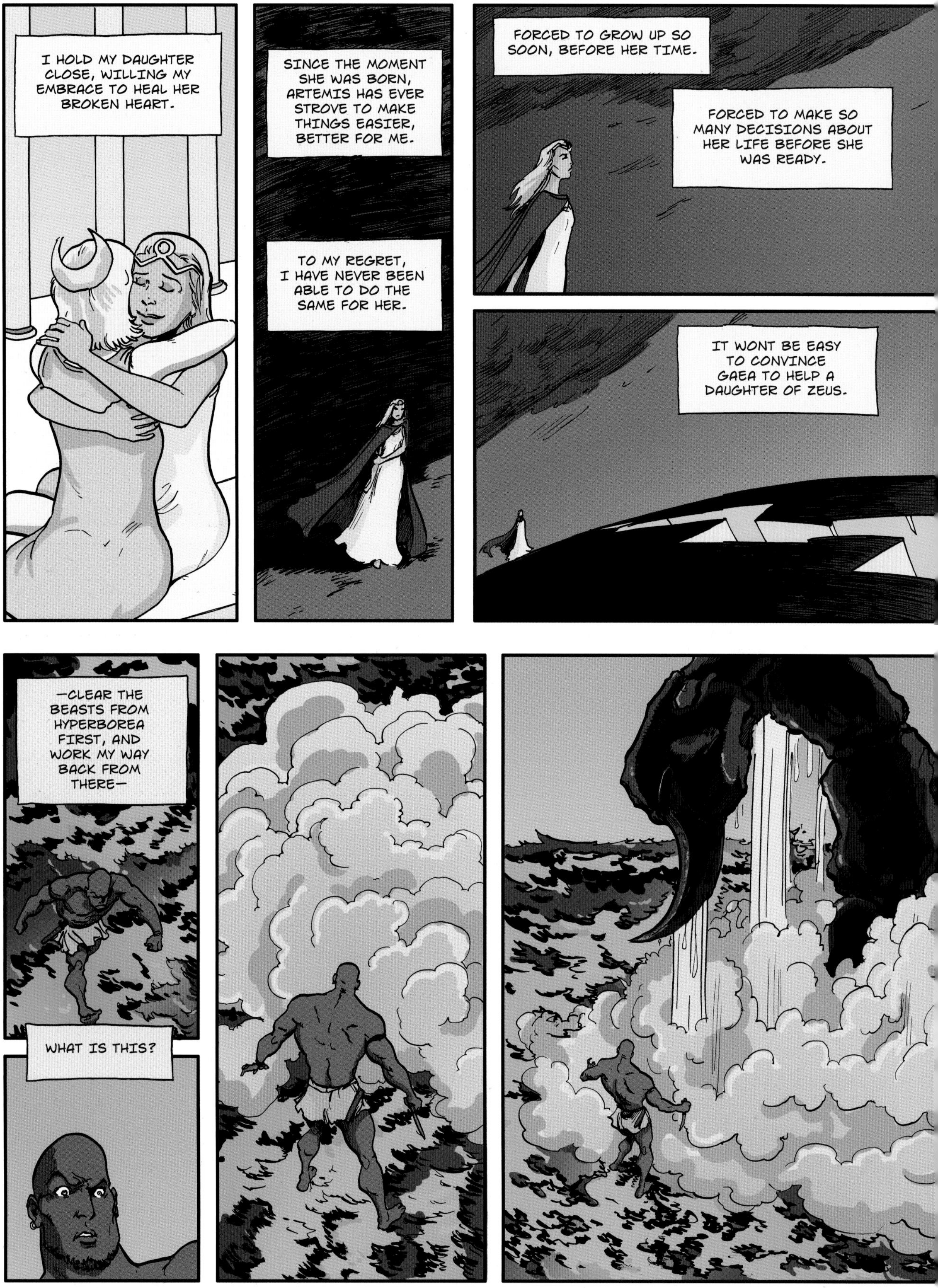
I HOLD MY DAUGHTER CLOSE, WILLING MY EMBRACE TO HEAL HER BROKEN HEART.
SINCE THE MOMENT SHE WAS BORN, ARTEMIS HAS EVER STROVE TO MAKE THINGS EASIER, BETTER FOR ME.
TO MY REGRET, I HAVE NEVER BEEN ABLE TO DO THE SAME FOR HER.
FORCED TO GROW UP SO SOON, BEFORE HER TIME.
FORCED TO MAKE SO MANY DECISIONS ABOUT HER LIFE BEFORE SHE WAS READY.
IT WONT BE EASY TO CONVINCE GAEA TO HELP A DAUGHTER OF ZEUS.
—CLEAR THE BEASTS FROM HYPERBOREA FIRST, AND WORK MY WAY BACK FROM THERE—
WHAT IS THIS?

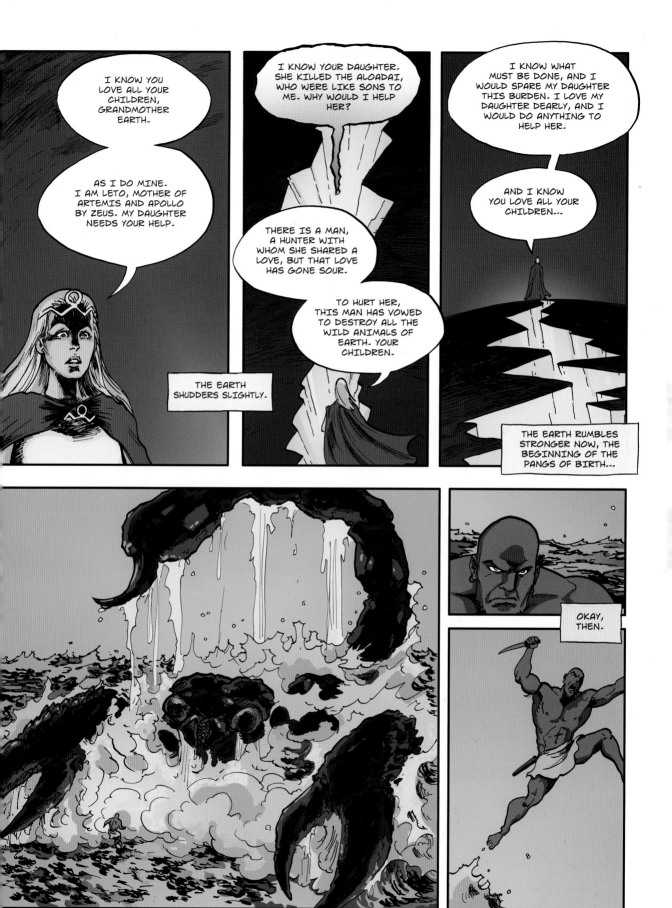

I KNOW YOU LOVE ALL YOUR CHILDREN, GRANDMOTHER EARTH.

AS I DO MINE. I AM LETO, MOTHER OF ARTEMIS AND APOLLO BY ZEUS. MY DAUGHTER NEEDS YOUR HELP.

I KNOW YOUR DAUGHTER. SHE KILLED THE ALOADAI, WHO WERE LIKE SONS TO ME. WHY WOULD I HELP HER?

THERE IS A MAN, A HUNTER WITH WHOM SHE SHARED A LOVE, BUT THAT LOVE HAS GONE SOUR.

TO HURT HER, THIS MAN HAS VOWED TO DESTROY ALL THE WILD ANIMALS OF EARTH. YOUR CHILDREN.

THE EARTH SHUDDERS SLIGHTLY.

I KNOW WHAT MUST BE DONE, AND I WOULD SPARE MY DAUGHTER THIS BURDEN. I LOVE MY DAUGHTER DEARLY, AND I WOULD DO ANYTHING TO HELP HER.

AND I KNOW YOU LOVE ALL YOUR CHILDREN...

THE EARTH RUMBLES STRONGER NOW, THE BEGINNING OF THE PANGS OF BIRTH...

OKAY, THEN.

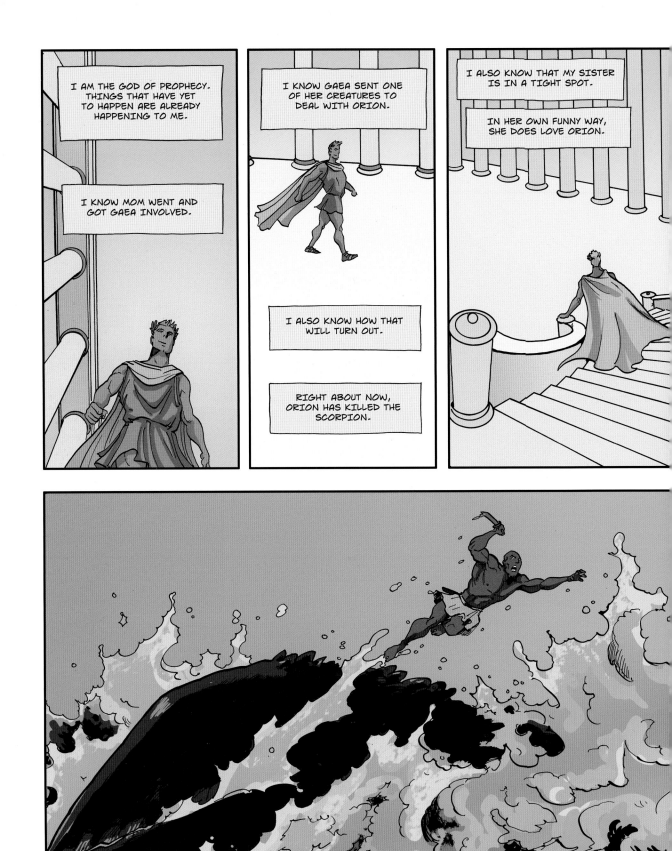

I AM THE GOD OF PROPHECY. THINGS THAT HAVE YET TO HAPPEN ARE ALREADY HAPPENING TO ME.

I KNOW MOM WENT AND GOT GAEA INVOLVED.

I KNOW GAEA SENT ONE OF HER CREATURES TO DEAL WITH ORION.

I ALSO KNOW HOW THAT WILL TURN OUT.

RIGHT ABOUT NOW, ORION HAS KILLED THE SCORPION.

I ALSO KNOW THAT MY SISTER IS IN A TIGHT SPOT.

IN HER OWN FUNNY WAY, SHE DOES LOVE ORION.

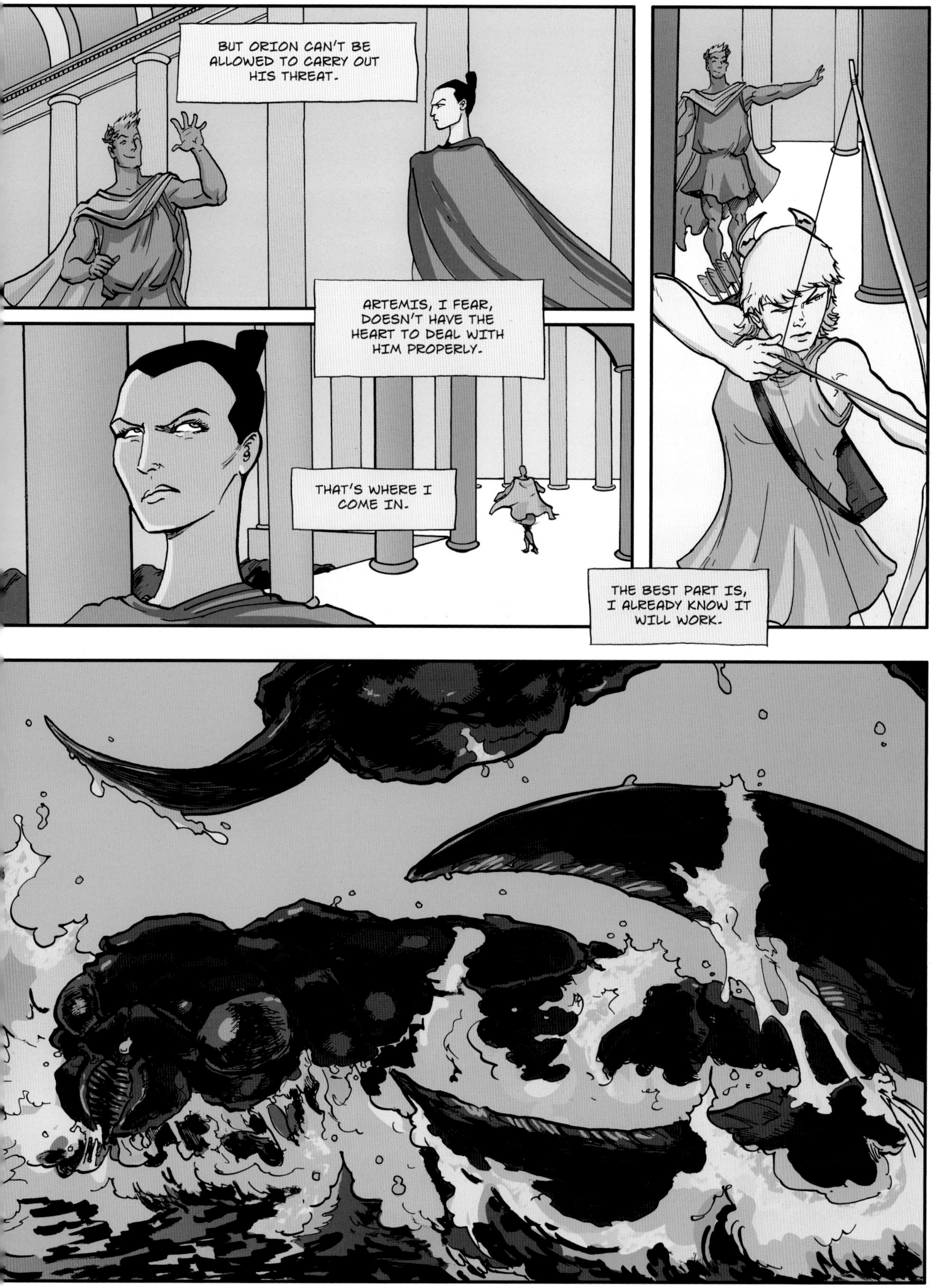
BUT ORION CAN'T BE ALLOWED TO CARRY OUT HIS THREAT.
ARTEMIS, I FEAR, DOESN'T HAVE THE HEART TO DEAL WITH HIM PROPERLY.
THAT'S WHERE I COME IN.
THE BEST PART IS, I ALREADY KNOW IT WILL WORK.

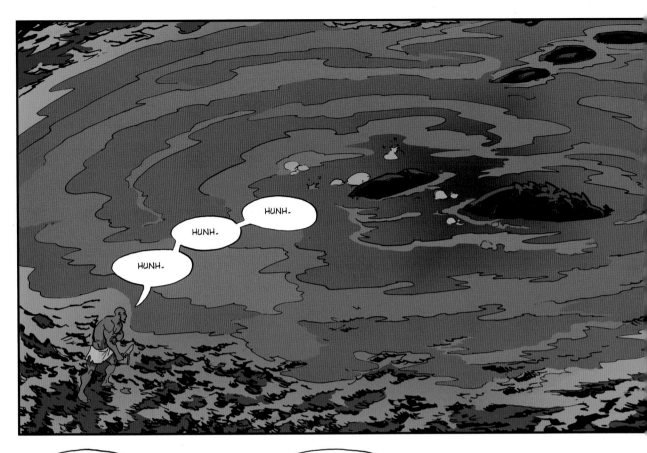

HUNH.

HUNH.

HUNH.

JUST WHO I WAS LOOKING FOR! WHAT ARE YOU DOING, MY SISTER?

SHOOTING, HUH? HOW ABOUT A LITTLE COMPETITION?

I SEE IT.

SHOOTING. THINKING.

SEE THAT GLEAMING SPECK ON THE HORIZON? THE SHELL OF A TURTLE I ESPIED EARLIER THIS MORNING.

HEH.

A TINY SPARKLING BEAD IN THE SEA.

DO YOU THINK YOU CAN HIT IT?

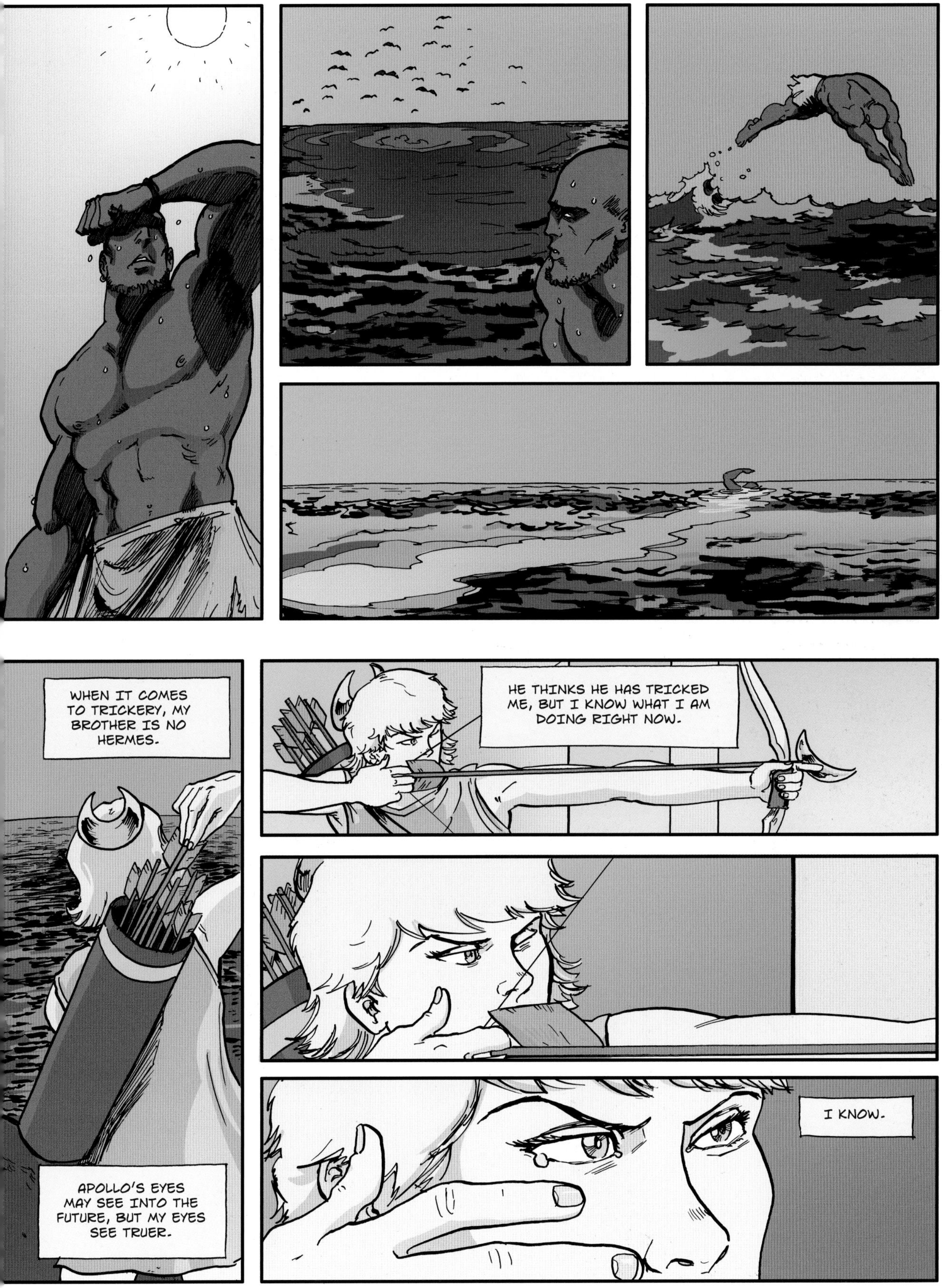
WHEN IT COMES TO TRICKERY, MY BROTHER IS NO HERMES.
HE THINKS HE HAS TRICKED ME, BUT I KNOW WHAT I AM DOING RIGHT NOW.
I KNOW.
APOLLO'S EYES MAY SEE INTO THE FUTURE, BUT MY EYES SEE TRUER.

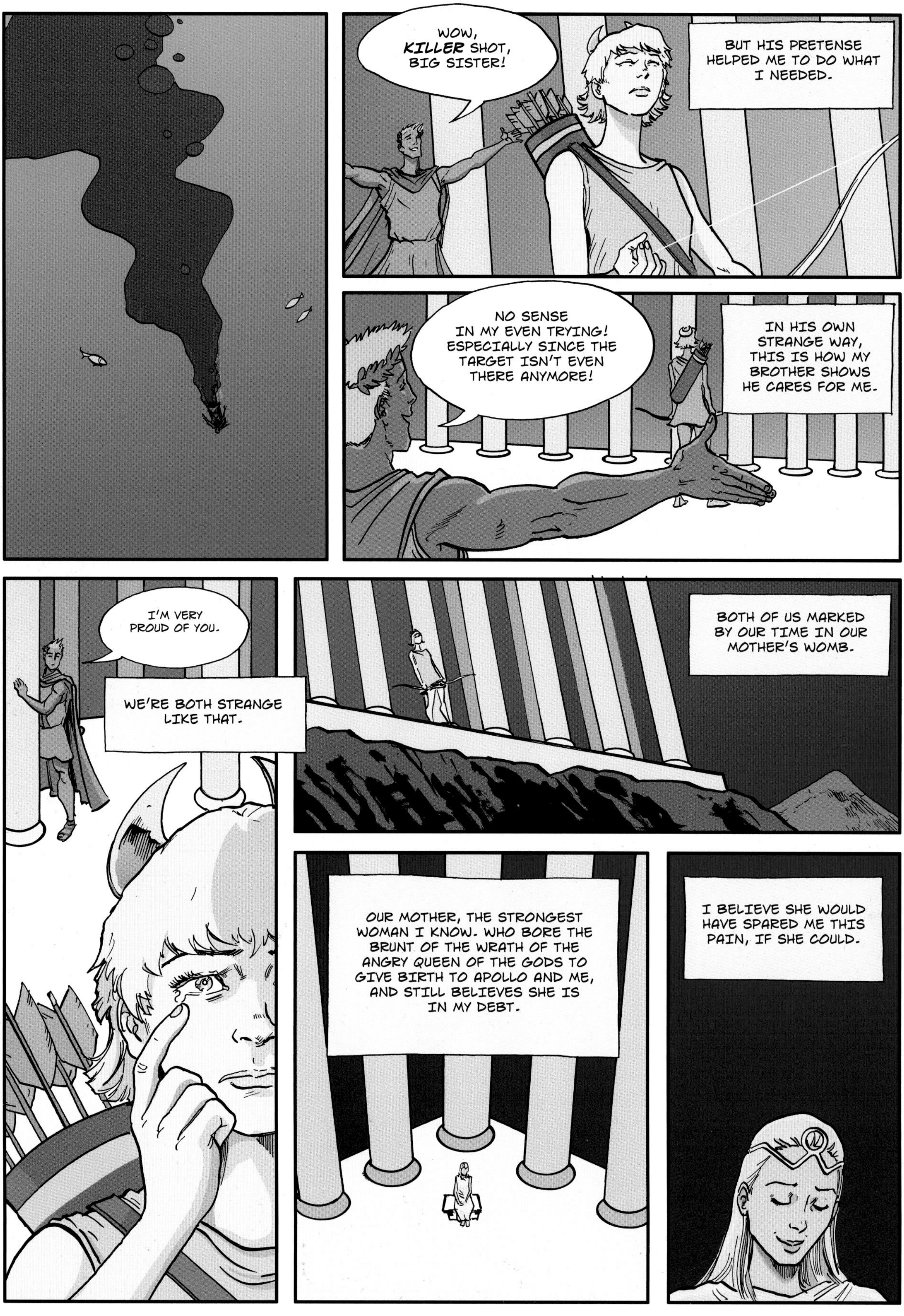
WOW, KILLER SHOT, BIG SISTER!
BUT HIS PRETENSE HELPED ME TO DO WHAT I NEEDED.
NO SENSE IN MY EVEN TRYING! ESPECIALLY SINCE THE TARGET ISN'T EVEN THERE ANYMORE!
IN HIS OWN STRANGE WAY, THIS IS HOW MY BROTHER SHOWS HE CARES FOR ME.
I'M VERY PROUD OF YOU.
WE'RE BOTH STRANGE LIKE THAT.
BOTH OF US MARKED BY OUR TIME IN OUR MOTHER'S WOMB.
OUR MOTHER, THE STRONGEST WOMAN I KNOW. WHO BORE THE BRUNT OF THE WRATH OF THE ANGRY QUEEN OF THE GODS TO GIVE BIRTH TO APOLLO AND ME, AND STILL BELIEVES SHE IS IN MY DEBT.
I BELIEVE SHE WOULD HAVE SPARED ME THIS PAIN, IF SHE COULD.

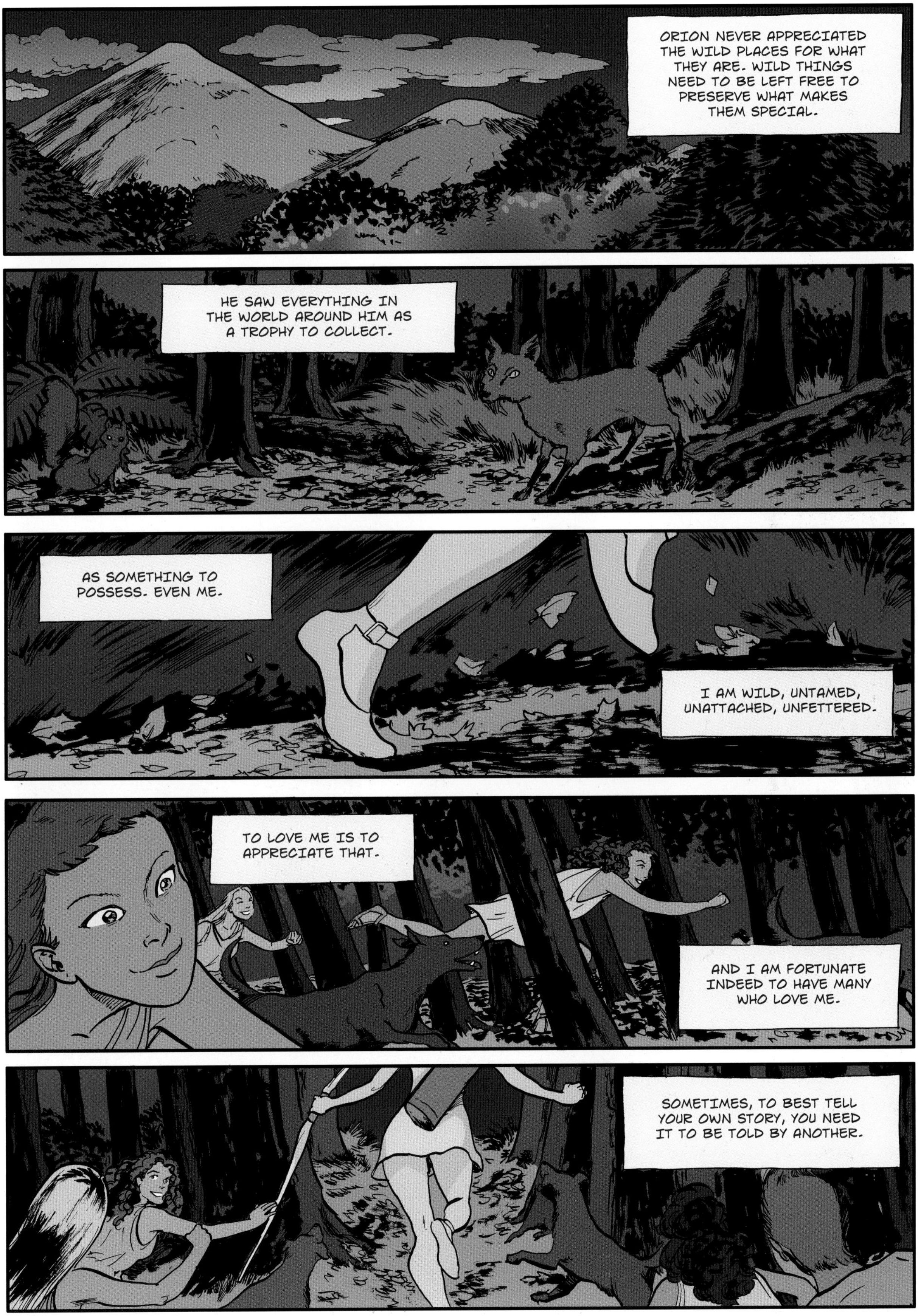
ORION NEVER APPRECIATED THE WILD PLACES FOR WHAT THEY ARE. WILD THINGS NEED TO BE LEFT FREE TO PRESERVE WHAT MAKES THEM SPECIAL.
HE SAW EVERYTHING IN THE WORLD AROUND HIM AS A TROPHY TO COLLECT.
AS SOMETHING TO POSSESS. EVEN ME.
I AM WILD, UNTAMED, UNATTACHED, UNFETTERED.
TO LOVE ME IS TO APPRECIATE THAT.
AND I AM FORTUNATE INDEED TO HAVE MANY WHO LOVE ME.
SOMETIMES, TO BEST TELL YOUR OWN STORY, YOU NEED IT TO BE TOLD BY ANOTHER.

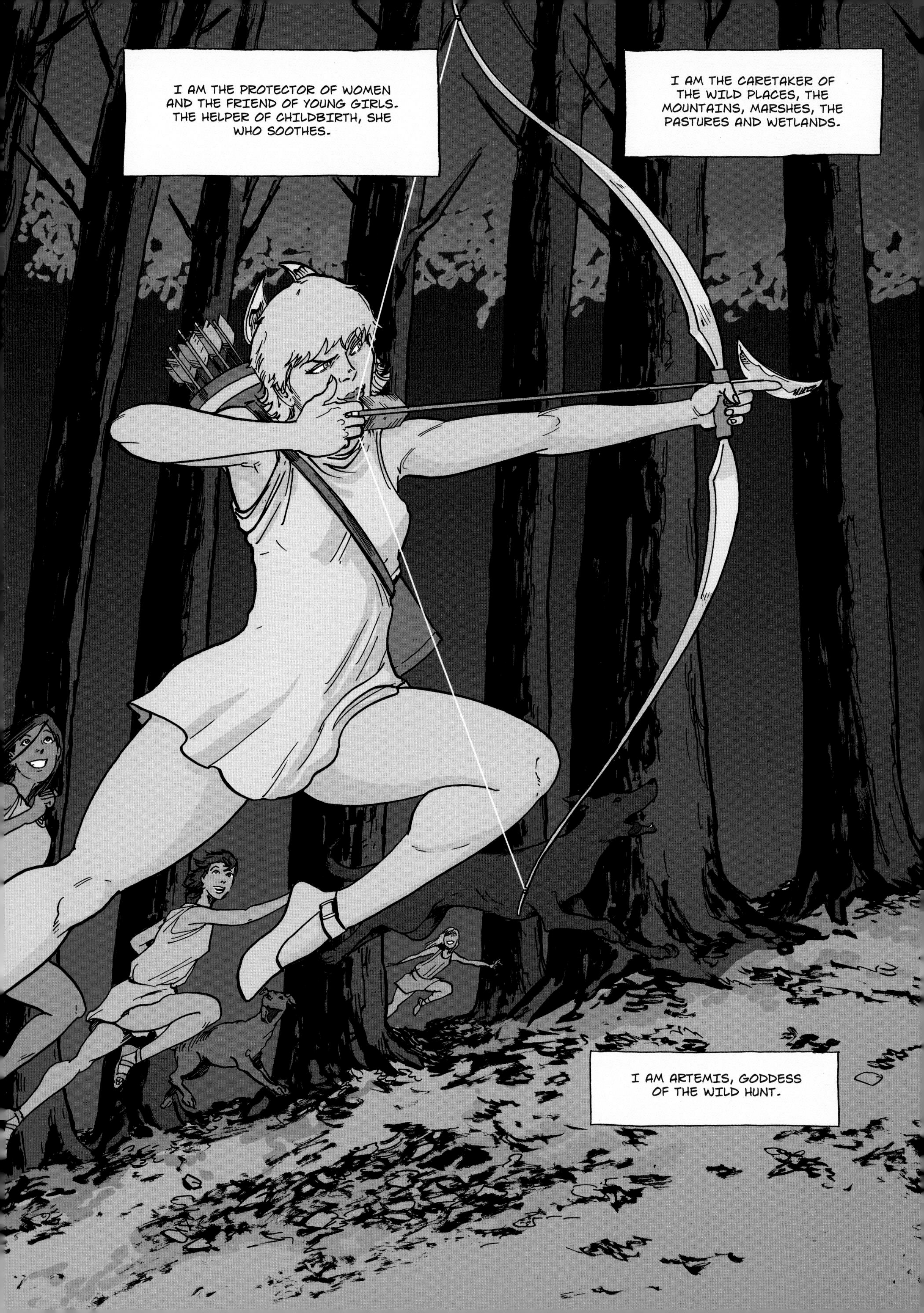
I AM THE PROTECTOR OF WOMEN AND THE FRIEND OF YOUNG GIRLS. THE HELPER OF CHILDBIRTH, SHE WHO SOOTHES.
I AM THE CARETAKER OF THE WILD PLACES, THE MOUNTAINS, MARSHES, THE PASTURES AND WETLANDS.
I AM ARTEMIS, GODDESS OF THE WILD HUNT.

AUTHOR'S NOTE

At this point we're getting to some of the books I was most excited for in OLYMPIANS. When I initially planned out the series, I saved some of my favorite gods and goddesses for toward the end, to make sure I had something to look forward to. And Artemis was, and is, definitely one of my favorites.

But why? What is the appeal of Artemis? She's not necessarily the nicest goddess. I mean, she certainly has a cruel streak—just look at poor Niobe. And she doesn't suffer fools gladly—look at her treatment of Actaeon, or even Orion. If I were to ever meet her somehow, in real life, I'm not confident it would go well. I'm pretty sure I'd inadvertently offend her and end up an arrow pincushion or torn apart by a pack of hunting dogs or something equally fatal.

What I think I dig about Artemis so much is that she has always known what she wants. Right from the start, when she first meets her father, Zeus, Artemis seems to have figured out who she will be, what she will do, and how to get there.

I may not share many qualities with Artemis, but this one key feature of her personality, at least, I feel a kinship with. When I was a little kid, about the same age as the gap-toothed little Artemis from this book, I knew that I wanted to grow up and tell stories, and to draw pictures. Lo and behold, all these years later, that's exactly what I do. I don't think this is indicative of any great quality in me, any superlative act of will or noble sense of purpose. I think I just realized early on who I would be, what I would do, and how to get there. Just like Artemis.

This book you're holding has been one of my favorites to create. Thanks to everyone who has made this journey with me so far.

George O'Connor
Brooklyn, NY
2016

ARTEMIS

WILD GODDESS OF THE HUNT

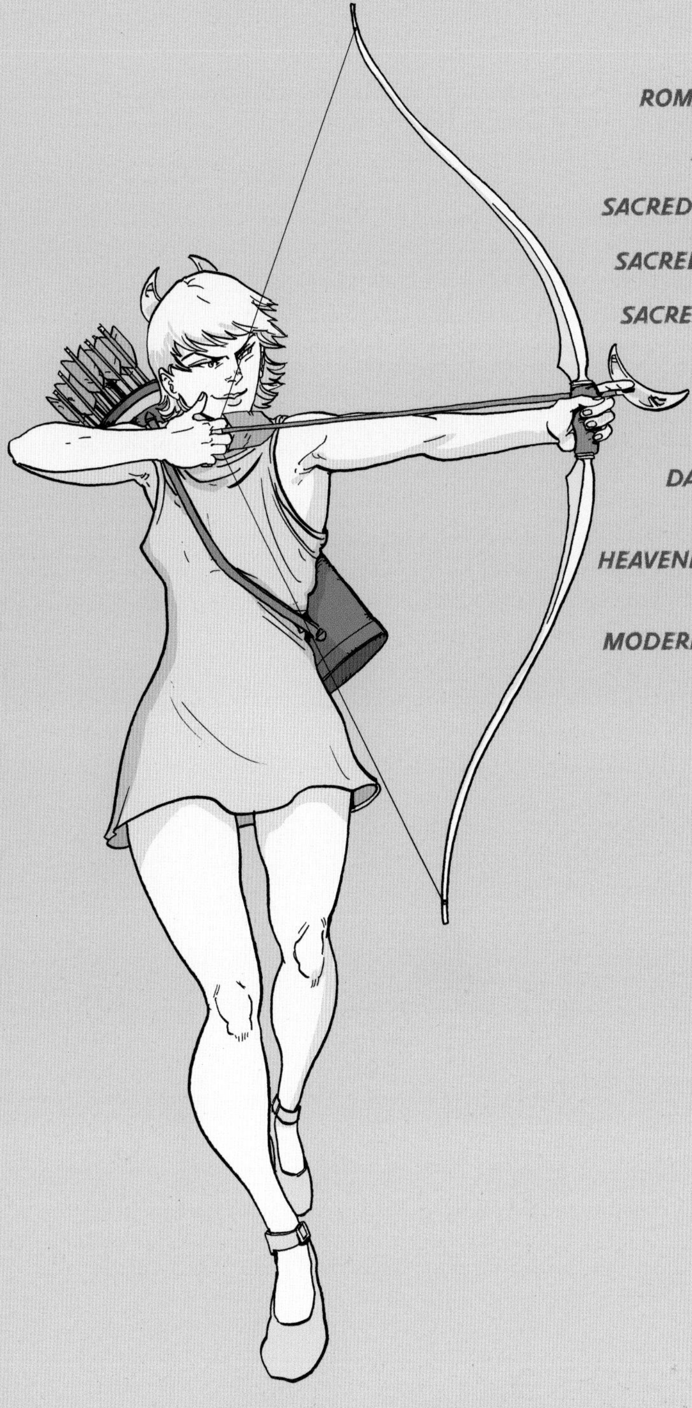

GODDESS OF	Hunting, Nature, Archery, Wild Animals, Girls, Young Women, Childbirth, Sudden Death; in later antiquity, the Moon
ROMAN NAME	Diana
SYMBOLS	Bow, Arrow, Crescent Moon
SACRED ANIMALS	Deer, Hunting Dog, Snake
SACRED PLANTS	Palm Tree, Amaranth, Cypress
SACRED PLACES	Delos (site of her birth); Arcadia (her favorite hunting grounds); Ephesus, Turkey (site of her temple that was one of the Seven Wonders of the Ancient World)
DAY OF THE WEEK	Monday (owing to her association with the moon)
HEAVENLY BODIES	The Moon; also the minor planet 105 Artemis and the asteroid 78 Diana
MODERN LEGACY	An entire genus of plants, Artemisia, takes its name from the goddess. The alcoholic beverage absinthe is made with the extract of one of these plants. Artemis's Roman name, Diana, remains a popular name to this day. Notable Dianas include Diana, the Princess of Wales, and Diana Prince, the civilian identity of comic book character Wonder Woman.

G^REEK NOTES

PAGE 1: The Muses sing the praises of Apollo in OLYMPIANS Book 8, *Apollo: The Brilliant One.*

PAGE 3, PANEL 1: There's that line again...

PAGE 3, PANEL 5: The agents of Hera are, from left to right, Iris, Ares, and Python. For another view of this tale see the aforementioned *Apollo: The Brilliant One.*

PAGE 5: I went back and forth so many times on how to depict newborn Artemis midwifing the birth of her twin brother. Finally I just went with showing wee baby Artemis Hulking herself out to toddler status. Thanks to Hazel Newlevant for that simple, elegant, and fun-to-draw idea.

PAGE 8, PANEL 1: The little gap in kid Artemis's teeth is my favorite thing.

PAGE 14, PANEL 3: Again, Apollo has his revenge on Python in OLYMPIANS Book 8, *Apollo: The Brilliant One.*

PAGE 15: I think Niobe is really missing the point in why the people worship Leto and not her. Quality, not quantity, Niobe!

PAGE 16, PANELS 3 AND 4: Read more about Tantalos, aka the worst host ever, in OLYMPIANS Book 4, *Hades: Lord of the Dead.*

PAGE 19, PANEL 4: And this story is why, when people ask me which god I'd least want to meet, I always say without hesitation "Apollo!" He edges out his sister because of his whole skinning-a-dude-alive-in-a-music-contest thing (again, see OLYMPIANS Book 8, *Apollo: The Brilliant One*). Compared to Artemis and Apollo, I think hanging out with Ares would be like a nice day in the park.

PAGE 19, PANEL 7: From time to time I like to add bits from lost Greek works into the text of OLYMPIANS. The line "Seated on their tomb, she made lament over her dead children" is a surviving fragment of a lost play about Niobe by Aeschylus.

PAGE 20, PANEL 7: If you ever happen to find yourself in Turkey, take a hike up Mount Sipylus and you can see this very formation. According to some sources, Niobe's rock, or the Weeping Rock as it is also known, still "cries" to this day. That may be because it is made of porous limestone, or it may be because this is a very sad story.

PAGE 21, PANEL 9: I was not able to determine what Actaeon meant; I'm positing here that it meant "creepy peeping Tom."

PAGE 26, PANEL 2: No, Actaeon! Not cool! Get out of there!

PAGE 27, PANEL 5: Welp, too late. Nice knowing you, Actaeon.

PAGE 32: We previously, very briefly, met Otus and Ephialtes in OLYMPIANS Book 5, *Poseidon: Earth Shaker.*

PAGE 35, PANEL 1: As the busiest god on Olympus, Hermes is, among many other things, the god of thieves, hence his comment here.

PAGE 35, PANEL 6: Turn to the front inside cover of this book, and take a gander at that family tree. Can you imagine how different it would look if these two stopped having kids?

PAGE 35, PANEL 7: The Gigantes attacked Olympus by stacking mountains atop one another in OLYMPIANS Book 2, *Athena: Grey-Eyed Goddess*. Not being born of Grandmother Earth directly, the Aloadai are not strictly speaking Gigantes, but if it looks like a duck...

PAGE 38, PANEL 1: Heracles had to capture the (real) Ceryneian Hind in OLYMPIANS Book 3, *Hera: The Goddess and Her Glory*. The Hind is a sibling to the four golden-horned stags who pull Artemis's chariot.

PAGE 41, PANEL 7: Fun with words, kids. Next time you have to tinkle in class, be sure to raise your hand and ask the teacher, "Excuse me, (sir or madam), I am afraid that I suddenly feel the pressing need to micturate. Might I please be excused from the lesson so that I may relieve this pressure and return my full attention to your teachings, forthwith?"

PAGE 42, PANEL 4: This really is a dirty job.

PAGE 42, PANEL 6: The Latin word for "urine" is *urina*, and it isn't too hard to see how they were able to equate that with Orion.

PAGE 44, PANELS 2–4: *Hippopotamus* is Greek for "river horse," which is why Orion calls it that. Alternately, I stuck with rhinoceros because calling it "nose horn" would make Orion sound like a weird caveman. Ancient Greeks called giraffes "leopard camels" and, really, I can see it.

Mythological-creature factoid lightning round! *Go!*

PAGE 44, PANEL 9: The Achlis has no joints in its hind legs, so it has to walk backward and eat grass with its trunk-like nose; PANEL 10: The Catoblepas's head is so heavy that it always looks down, which is fortunate as its gaze is deadly; PANEL 11: The Bonosos was a type of buffalo who could protect itself with expulsions of burning excrement that could shoot up to 700 feet.

PAGE 45, PANEL 1: The Eale has huge horns that can swivel to point forward when it's threatened; PANEL 2: The Leucocrotta has a wide-opening mouth, bony ridges instead of teeth, and is able to mimic human voices in order to lure potential prey into the woods; PANEL 3: The Gorilla is—hey, gorillas are real! Why are they here with all these mythical creatures? Well, gorillas were first named and described by Hanno the Navigator in approximately 500 BCE, but were thought to be mythical beasts in the West until 1848; PANEL 4: Dragons are a very obscure type of mythological creature that almost no one has ever heard of, so let's move on; PANEL 5: Gryphons are ferocious beasts who were thought to guard both golden hoards and Leto's homeland of Hyperborea. There is an interesting modern theory that the Gryphon was inspired by ancients finding fossilized skeletons of the beaked dinosaur Protoceratops; PANEL 6: The Manticore is a freaky beast with three rows of teeth, a human face, and a scorpion's tale. Like the Leucocrotta, it lures victims away with mimicked human speech; PANEL 9: This is a Unicorn, another mythical beast that almost no one has ever heard of.

PAGE 47, PANEL 4: One last monster—the Ketea Indikoi, a group of whale-like creatures living in the Indian Ocean who have strange terrestrial-animal heads (in this instance, that of a ram).

PAGE 50: Atalanta has a pretty good superhero origin story. In my opinion, "raised by bears" is as valid a reason for superpowers as "bitten by radioactive spider" or "splashed by chemicals and hit by lightning." I mean, both of those are just going to make you dead. You might actually survive being raised by bears.

PAGE 51, PANEL 5: The three cult statues with offerings before that are Demeter, Persephone, and Dionysos. As all three gods are associated with the harvest, it makes sense that King Oineus would be extra careful to not short them, but to ignore Artemis?! Did he not see what happened with Niobe?

PAGE 51, PANEL 8: We first met Theseus in OLYMPIANS Book 5, *Poseidon: Earth Shaker*. He is getting a dirty look from the dioscuri, Castor and Polydeuces, whom we briefly saw, along with Atalanta, in OLYMPIANS Book 3, *Hera: The Goddess and Her Glory*, where they were all depicted as members of Jason's Argonauts. Castor and Polydeuces are no doubt mad at Theseus because he had carried off their baby sister Helen, she of future Trojan War fame, after he'd heard from an oracle that she was going to grow up to be real pretty. Theseus is a major creep. Also seen here are Heracles's mortal twin Iphicles (last seen as a baby in *Hera*), with son Iolaus, who is still apparently going on about that time he helped Uncle Heracles with the torch against the Hydra. Give it a rest, Iolaus.

PAGE 55, PANEL 1: The two scowling gentlemen in the foreground are Meleager's brothers, who are upset at Meleager for giving the prize to a woman. This eventually leads to very bad things, for them and Meleager.

PAGE 55, PANEL 6: I kind of hate the story of Atalanta and the race of the golden apples, and not just because I worked for many years in a children's bookstore where I heard the "Free to Be You and Me" version of this story, like, three times a day. Dude, if you have to cheat with magical apples to get a woman to marry you, you'll never really win. Loser.

PAGE 57: Leto dropping some real truth bombs here.

PAGES 58–64: There are several accounts of how Orion met his end, all valid, and this was my way of addressing them all. I felt it was most important that Artemis have her own agency and deal with him knowingly, but I love the trickery of Apollo too much not to reference it. That's so Apollo. And the scorpion is where we get the zodiac sign of Scorpio from. Scorpio is the best sign of the zodiac. I myself am a Scorpio, and if you disagree with me, I'll pinch you with my claws and sting you with my venomous tail.

LETO
MOTHER OF ARTEMIS AND APOLLO

GODDESS OF Motherhood, Demureness

ROMAN NAME Latona

SYMBOLS Bow, Arrow, Crescent Moon

SACRED ANIMAL Wolf (the form she took to hide from Hera)

SACRED PLANT Palm Tree

SACRED PLACES Delos (site of her birth of the divine twins), along with most temples to her children

HEAVENLY BODIES Minor planet 639 Latona and asteroid 68 Leto

ORION
THE MIGHTY HUNTER

SACRED PLACES   Boiotia (site of birth), Chios, Sicily

HEAVENLY BODIES   The constellation Orion, one of the most famous and easy-to-identify constellations. It contains the very bright stars Rigel and Betelgeuse (Betelgeuse! Betelgeuse!).

Additionally, the constellation of Scorpio, named after the scorpion that in some accounts kills him, follows the constellation of Orion through the sky.

MODERN LEGACY   In addition to his eponymous constellation, the name Orion crops up a lot in space stuff, as a series of satellites, an upcoming manned spacecraft, and as the name of the lunar module for the Apollo 16 mission, among others.

Orion has also lent his name to the DC comics superhero created by Jack Kirby, and Orion Pictures was a movie studio that produced many of the films of Woody Allen, among others.

ABOUT THIS BOOK

ARTEMIS: GODDESS OF THE WILD HUNT is the ninth book in
OLYMPIANS, a graphic novel series from First Second that retells the
Greek myths.

FOR DISCUSSION

1 When Artemis meets her dad, Zeus, for the first time, he asks her what gifts she
wants from him. What would you ask, if you had the chance?

2 Artemis can be very cruel. Do you think she and Apollo are justified in what they
do to Niobe and her children? How about what she does to Actaeon?

3 What do you think Leto said to Niobe on Mount Sipylus before she transformed her?

4 Artemis was not originally a goddess of the moon. Why do you think she became
associated with the moon? How does Selene fit into all of this?

5 Who is a bigger creep, Actaeon or Orion?

6 Who would you rather spend a day with, Artemis or Apollo?

7 Why do you think Artemis wanted to become the goddess of the hunt? And why do
you think she never wants to marry?

8 Very few people believe in the Greek gods today. Why do you think it's important
that we still learn about them?

BIBLIOGRAPHY

APOLLODORUS, THE LIBRARY, VOLUME 1.
PSEUDO-APOLLODORUS, NEW YORK: LOEB CLASSICAL LIBRARY, 1921.
Apollodorus, or pseudo-Apollodorus, *whoever you really are*, was my main source for the Aloadai giants.

CALLIMACHUS: HYMNS AND EPIGRAMS, LYCOPHRON AND ARATUS.
CALLIMACHUS, NEW YORK: LOEB CLASSICAL LIBRARY, 1921.
I really like the writings of Callimachus. His Hymn to Artemis was the primary source I used for the childhood of Artemis, as well as the account of her first four arrows.

HOMERIC HYMNS. HOMERIC APOCRYPHA. LIVES OF HOMER.
EDITED AND TRANSLATED BY M L WEST. LOEB CLASSICAL LIBRARY. CAMBRIDGE, MA: HARVARD UNIVERSITY PRESS, 2007.
I used the Homeric Hymn to Apollo contained within this collection as a source for the birth of Apollo and his slaying of the serpent Python.

METAMORPHOSES. OVID. TRANSLATED BY DAVID RAEBURN. NEW YORK: PENGUIN CLASSICS, 2004.
Metamorphoses is a Roman text, so Artemis is called Diana within. It's a really fun read, and I used Ovid's accounts of Niobe and Actaeon as my primary source for those stories.

THEOI GREEK MYTHOLOGY WEB SITE WWW.THEOI.COM
Without a doubt, the single most valuable resource I came across in this entire venture. At Theoi.com, you can find an encyclopedia of various gods and goddesses from Greek mythology, cross referenced with every mention of them they could find in literally hundreds of ancient Greek and Roman texts. Unfortunately, it's not quite complete, and it doesn't seem to be updated anymore.

WWW.LIBRARY.THEOI.COM
A subsection of the above site, it's an online archive of hundreds of ancient Greek and Roman texts. Many of these have never been published in the traditional sense, and many are just fragments recovered from ancient papyrus, or recovered text from other authors' quotations of lost epics. Invaluable.

MYTH INDEX WEB SITE WWW.MYTHINDEX.COM
Another mythology Web site connected to Theoi.com. While it doesn't have the painstakingly compiled quotations from ancient texts, it does offer some impressive encyclopedic entries on virtually every character to ever pass through a Greek myth. Pretty amazing.

ALSO RECOMMENDED
FOR YOUNGER READERS

D'Aulaires' Book of Greek Myths. Ingri and Edgar Parin D'Aulaire. New York: Doubleday, 1962.

Artemis the Brave. Joan Holub. New York: Simon and Schuster, 2010.

FOR OLDER READERS

The Marriage of Cadmus and Harmony. Robert Calasso. New York: Knopf, 1993.

Mythology. Edith Hamilton. New York: Grand Central Publishing, 1999.

ATALANTA

SWIFT HUNTRESS

MEANING OF NAME "Equal in weight," because she was the equal of any man

SACRED ANIMALS Bear, Lion

SACRED PLANTS Not sacred to her per se, Atalanta is associated with the golden apple that Hippomenes (or Melanion) used to defeat her in the famous footrace

SACRED PLACES Arcadia (the site of many of her adventures), the island of Atalanta off the coast of Boiotia, the island of Atalanta off the coast of Athens

HEAVENLY BODY 36 Atalante, an asteroid

For Artamiss

—G.O.

First Second

New York

Copyright © 2017 by George O'Connor

Published by First Second
First Second is an imprint of Roaring Brook Press,
a division of Holtzbrinck Publishing Holdings Limited Partnership
120 Broadway, New York, NY 10271

Library of Congress Control Number: 2016938491

Paperback ISBN: 978-1-62672-522-5
Hardcover ISBN: 978-1-62672-521-8

Our books may be purchased in bulk for promotional, educational, or business use. Please contact your
local bookseller or the Macmillan Corporate and Premium Sales Department at (800) 221-7945 ext.
5442 or by e-mail at MacmillanSpecialMarkets@macmillan.com.

First Edition 2017

Book design by Rob Steen

Printed in China by Toppan Leefung Printing Ltd., Dongguan City, Guangdong Province

Paperback: 10 9 8 7
Hardcover: 10 9 8 7 6 5 4